"I'll behave as I see fit," Vicky said

"You may be filling my father's place, but I can assure you it's strictly temporary!"

"Well..." Scott drawled, smiling lazily, "we'll just leave that little decision up to him, shall we? Hmm?"

Vicky's face burned with anger. She said shakily, "You think you're pretty hot stuff, don't you? But I'm not taking any orders from you."

He laughed, sliding his hands into his pockets and eyeing her in mocking silence.

"You may have wormed your way into Daddy's affections," she went on angrily, "but I can see straight through you and you're not phoneying your way into mine!"

He watched her coolly. "You, Prodigal Daughter—me, Wicked Usurper?"

"Upstart," she said flatly, "is the word I would have chosen."

After going to school in London, English writer **SARAH HOLLAND** struck out on her own. She worked in various offices around London, and also as a singer in a recording studio, until illness forced her to return to her family, who had moved to the Isle of Man. There she started writing for Harlequin, and though her first book, according to Sarah, was not very good, she was encouraged to keep on. Her second book, *Too Hot to Handle,* was accepted immediately, and since then she has had more than seven novels published. Though she's interested in theater and has taken a course at a drama school in London, she says she will continue to write romance novels.

Books by Sarah Holland

HARLEQUIN PRESENTS
516—TOO HOT TO HANDLE
536—TOMORROW BEGAN YESTERDAY
552—THE DEVIL'S MISTRESS
576—DEADLY ANGEL
601—FEVER PITCH
1192—THE HEAT IS ON

HARLEQUIN ROMANCE
2705—BLUEBEARD'S BRIDE

Don't miss any of our special offers. Write to us at the following address for information on our newest releases.

Harlequin Reader Service
P.O. Box 1397, Buffalo, NY 14240
Canadian address: P.O. Box 603,
Fort Erie, Ont. L2A 5X3

SARAH HOLLAND

an adult love

Harlequin Books

TORONTO • NEW YORK • LONDON
AMSTERDAM • PARIS • SYDNEY • HAMBURG
STOCKHOLM • ATHENS • TOKYO • MILAN

Harlequin Presents first edition August 1991
ISBN 0-373-11387-0

Original hardcover edition published in 1990
by Mills & Boon Limited

AN ADULT LOVE

CHAPTER ONE

THE noisy, crowded club echoed with the heavy thud of a bass guitar, and Vicky looked up once more from her table, disliking the act intensely. It could go on for another hour and still not improve, she knew that without question. They were a bad group, with a bad set, and a truly appalling lead vocalist. What was more, they almost totally ruined the atmosphere of Chaingang's, the top London venue for new, unsigned acts. Normally Vicky would enjoy her evening here enormously, watching the bright young talent of London working against a backdrop of red-brick walls, stark wooden tables and chairs. Tonight she just felt bored and restless and fed up.

'Another drink?' Spike indicated her glass, one arched brow raised.

Vicky shook her black head. 'I'd rather go, to be honest.' Her dark eyes slid around the club and she sighed. 'I think Jason picked a loser here. This band's never going to get anywhere.'

'I agree,' Spike said, nodding, and stood up. 'Come on. I'll drive you home.'

They left the club, walking across cobbled alleys past the cool, dark waters of Camden Lock, and headed down towards the rabbit warren of backstreets behind the market.

Vicky had been working for Timepiece Music for just over a year now, and part of her job was to attend gigs of unsigned bands in these London venues. She frequently went with Spike, who also worked for Timepiece, and although their reports were unofficial they were listened to with interest by their bosses, who were always on the lookout for fresh talent.

Spike unlocked the car, his tall, slim body striking in the semi-darkness. He looked a little like a borzoi, with his long, silky blond hair, long, thin nose and nervous movements.

'Had a phone call from my parents today,' he said as they drove home together. 'They went on at me to get a proper job and leave the music business alone.'

Vicky smiled. 'Parents!' Her voice attempted camaraderie, but it was only an act. Her mother had died when she was six years old, but her relationship with her father had been a disaster. She hadn't spoken to him for five years.

'They're acting in my best interests,' Spike said wryly, 'or so they keep telling me.'

'The usual propaganda,' Vicky said, and that was no act. Her father had spent years dominating her life, pressuring her with outbursts of frightening rage, trying to squeeze her into a box marked 'perfect daughter'. She had tried very hard to live up to his expectations. But when the box eventually grew too suffocating she had smashed it to pieces and walked away without a backward glance.

'Girlfriends were mentioned, of course,' Spike said.

'Of course,' Vicky said vaguely, looking out at London, glad of its anonymity, its facelessness, its freedom. No boxes for her to squeeze into here. No unrelenting pressure to make her perfect. Here, she could just hide away from all of that, take jobs when she wanted them, and live as though she weren't a Foxdale of Challarran.

'They want to meet you,' Spike said, and his voice broke into her thoughts. 'I don't suppose you'd be interested in Sunday lunch in Hampshire this weekend?'

She turned, studying him with dark eyes. The wind whipped her black hair against her white face, the open window letting in the cold, making her pull the scarlet coat around her white throat.

Spike glanced at her. 'No?'

She bit her lip. 'Well . . . I thought we'd agreed we were just friends, Spike?'

He nodded. 'We had.'

'So this invitation doesn't mean anything?'

Spike's thin mouth curved. 'It means I'd love to be invited in for coffee . . .' The car slowed outside her flat in the quiet tree-lined street, and Vicky watched him as he switched off the engine and turned to her. 'We've been seeing each other for six months, Vicky. Don't you think we should move away from first base?'

She cleared her throat, smiling. 'What's first base?' she asked, keeping her voice light and casual.

'This,' Spike said. 'This endless social contact with very little physical contact, which in reality is no contact at all.'

Vicky lowered her lashes. 'I see. You want to seduce me.'

He laughed, thin brows rising. 'What an invitation!' Then he was opening his car door, stepping out, and Vicky bit her lip, realising he'd taken her light words too seriously. Now how was she going to get out of this?

Following him up the path to the rambling Victorian house her flat was in, she racked her brains for a suitable put-down, but didn't have the heart to deliver it at the door. She'd have to explain once they were inside. He'd be humiliated if he realised she'd been teasing him.

She opened the front door and stepped in, waiting while he came in too. 'I'll make some coffee,' she told him warily. 'You go in and sit down.'

He caught her wrist, smiling. 'You don't seriously think I want any coffee, do you?'

Vicky stiffened. 'Spike . . .'

'Not with you here alone with me,' he said under his breath. 'Do you realise this is the first time we've been alone?' He drew her closer, eyes flickering over her white face. 'Isn't that incredible? How do you do it?'

'Do what?' she asked, puzzled, trying to think of a way to get out of his unwanted embrace without upsetting him.

'Keep all of us at a distance,' he said, his face buried in her dark hair, breathing in her scent, 'God, you smell gorgeous! Is that apple shampoo?'

Vicky frowned, trying to draw away from him. 'What do you mean—all? Who is "all of us"?'

He laughed, hands sliding on to her waist. 'All your escorts, Vicky. Me, Pete, Tony, Jeff—God knows how many more you've got stashed away. We're getting to the stage now where bets are being made to see which one of us you actually want!' His eyes danced at her and he added in what he presumably considered to be a sexy voice, 'I reckon I win hands down, because you spend more time with me than the others.'

She stared at him, incredulous. 'But they're just friends!' It was like being slapped in the face, hearing all those unwanted truths pouring out of him. He couldn't be serious. They were just colleagues, just friends, and the other men he had guessed at so accurately were also just friends. Men who lived close by and were involved in the arts. Ted, whom she'd met at her art evening class, and Phil, who was in a local band.

'Come on, Vicky,' he said with sudden dry cynicism, 'you don't fool me.' The dark eyes flickered over her with a sexual appraisal she had never seen in him before. 'You're as sexy as hell! Look at the clothes you wear—miniskirts and high heels and tight sweaters. Any man with half an eye can see you need a man around you almost constantly. I certainly can!'

'No!' she heard herself say in shock. 'No . . . you're wrong. My clothes are what everyone's wearing. I just like to be in fashion . . .' She stared down at herself, at the black polo-neck sweater, the black and white checked miniskirt and black high heels.

His brows rose in disbelief. 'Liar! I know what you want.' And the next second she was being pushed roughly against the banisters, and his mouth was sliding over hers.

Vicky stared at him, eyes wide, so stunned that she didn't move for a second. The kiss was passionate on his side. It was indifferent on hers. She stood passively, considering what on earth she could do, reeling under the weight of information he'd given her.

The boys at work? Taking bets on her? It was like having her whole world ripped up in front of her eyes. They were just friends—weren't they?

'Oh, Vicky . . .' he was saying under his breath as he grew more excited, unaware or uncaring that Vicky simply stood with her eyes open, unmoving.

She felt his hand at her breast and gasped, jerking into action, pulling away. 'Don't!' she burst out.

He stared, flushed, then his mouth tightened and he pulled her back roughly, making her cry out as her head hit the banister. 'Keep still,' he muttered. 'I'm sick of you teasing me! Do you think I can't see what you're doing? Walking the way you do? Showing yourself off? Telling me how good I look when we're out?' His hand was suddenly at her breast again, aggressive, hurting her deliberately. 'Either you're the nastiest little bitch I've ever met, or you want me to force you.' His mouth bruised hers in a punishing kiss as he whispered, 'Delighted, Vicky. Absolutely delighted.'

'Stop it!' She was struggling before she realised it, hitting him, a scuffle breaking out between them, silent and angry and growing dangerous as each wrestled with the realisation that a very big misunderstanding had been made on both sides.

'Spike! Don't!' Vicky gasped, half angry, half scared as he pinned her arms behind her back. 'You're hurting me!'

'Good! Women like you deserve to be——'

The living-room door opened. Their flushed faces turned, one embarrassed, one breathing angrily. Vicky had expected to see Josephine. The shock of the tall, dark man looming in the doorway took her breath away.

'Leave the lady alone,' a biting voice from her childhood said.

Vicky stared as Scott Thornton stepped forwards, out of the past and into the present, threat emanating from every line of that lean, hard body. His face was a threat in itself, carved from steel and razor-blades, grey eyes heavily lidded and cynical, his mouth a hard, uncompromising line.

Spike stared too, his heartbeat unsteady. 'Who the hell are you?'

'I'm the man who's going to knock your teeth out,' Scott drawled with soft menace, legs apart in a gesture of masculine authority that sent a quiver of fear through Vicky, let alone Spike, who held his breath and looked at her, alarmed.

'Who is he?' Spike asked in a half-whisper.

She was about to say in a rush that she hadn't seen him since she was six years old, that he'd been one of the most glamorous and exciting figures of her childhood, and that she had absolutely no idea what he was doing here.

'I'm her lover,' Scott said before she could speak. 'And I'm a very jealous man.' He was advancing slowly, grey eyes narrowed, and Spike released Vicky, backing, eyes wide. 'I like to pin her arms behind her back, too, but I only do it in the privacy of our bedroom, and then I do it three or four times a night.'

Spike was fumbling for the door-handle. 'My mistake,' he blabbered. 'It won't happen a——'

Scott's hand shot out around his throat, pinned him to the door. 'I'm a sadist,' he whispered on a deadly note of dark excitement, and smiled as Spike's eyes grew terrified. 'I like hurting people.

It turns me on.'

Spike was nodding, saying, 'Yes, yes, of course, I see, it won't happen again——'

'Good,' Scott purred, nodding, smiling like a madman. 'Good.' He opened the door with his other hand and manoeuvred Spike by the throat in one cold, clear movement on to the doorstep before slamming the door in his face.

Vicky listened as Spike ran to his car, and her eyes met Scott's in grateful anger. 'I don't believe you did that.'

Scott laughed, leaning on the door, sliding his hands into the pockets of his black trousers. 'Did you see his face!' The grey eyes glittered with wicked humour. 'Oh, God, if only it were on film!'

Vicky folded her arms, too grateful for her narrow escape to shout at him for ruining both her friendship and her reputation. 'What are you doing here, Scott? How on earth did you get my address?'

He pushed away from the door, coming towards her. 'Aren't you glad to see me?' he asked coolly, one dark brow raised. His glance flicked down over her body. 'I must say,' he drawled, 'I see what he means about the clothes. I remember you in pigtails and white socks. I hardly expected to find a siren in black stockings and a miniskirt.'

Vicky's face ran with hot colour and she moved away from him, folding her arms. 'And I remember you in jeans and a black leather jacket!' she said defensively, eyeing his expensive black cashmere coat, the dark suit he wore beneath it, the red silk tie and tight black waistcoat. 'Am I to assume your black motorbike isn't parked outside at the moment?'

He gave a slow, sardonic smile. 'Correct,' he drawled, 'I sold the bike and bought a Ferrari with the small change.'

Vicky clucked her tongue. 'Be serious!'

He eyed her coolly. 'Take a look. It's parked just up the street.'

She studied him for a moment, then decided she didn't care if he was telling her the truth, because she suddenly felt much more relaxed, and the relief of escape from Spike was fading fast.

Now that she felt better able to think, she was thinking fast. He couldn't have got her address from her family. Her family did not know where she lived—she'd made damn sure of that. Either he had hired a private detective to find her, or he had had her traced by the police.

Scott was watching her, his grey eyes intent. 'You're thinking,' he said under his breath. 'Don't think. Go in and sit down. I have something to tell you.'

Fear struck her heart and she felt suddenly weak, staring at his hard, familiar, exciting face. 'Something's happened . . .' she heard herself say huskily, and as she said it she knew it was true, panic making her heart skip like a rabbit. 'Has there been an accident . . .?'

He was silent, his face deadly serious. 'Go in

and sit down, Vicky.'

'Scott . . .' she said, sick, frightened, and allowed him to take her wrist and lead her into the living-room. Every stick of furniture was blindingly vivid: the gold mirror on the wall, her paintings hanging at odd intervals, the plant on the Japanese coffee-table, the photograph of Josephine's boyfriend on the dusty television.

'Sit,' he said deeply.

Mute, she shook her head. Her hand clung to his when he would have let go. She couldn't speak.

Scott gently pushed her into a chair, sat beside her. 'It's your father, Vicky,' he said deeply, watching the blood drain from her face. 'He's had a heart attack. He's not dead, don't worry, but it is serious, and you must come back to Challarran tonight.'

'Heart attack?' she repeated stupidly. Her father was seriously ill? He was ill and he had the Foxdale clan perched around him like vultures, desperate to get their hands on the money, the house, the business.

Her skin broke out in a cold sweat. 'When did it happen?'

'This afternoon,' Scott said. 'I was with him in the boardroom. We were alone. He was signing some papers. He gasped, put a hand to his chest . . .' The grey eyes flickered over her, saw her mouth tremble with the shock. 'I don't need to go into detail. It was very fast. Not much time to suffer. We were in the ambulance before——'

Her mind was spinning, listening to his cool, calm words with one half of her brain, the other fighting desperately not to lose control as she felt her two worlds collide with an impact that left her breathless, as though she were a train suddenly forced to change tracks and hurtle off towards self-destruction.

Back to Challarran? She couldn't go back. Her father hated her. He'd disinherited her five years ago, thrown her out of Challa and disowned her. As for the rest of the family—she was just a nuisance, the heiress who wouldn't play ball, wouldn't let them manipulate her to their own ends, and wouldn't squeeze herself into the straitjacket marked Future Mistress of Challa.

'He won't see me,' she said on a fierce whisper, interrupting Scott. 'Believe me, I know him. He won't see me!'

'He asked for you,' Scott said, dark brows rising.

There was a stunned silence. She stared at him, eyes very dark. 'He asked for me?' she repeated dumbly. 'Are you sure?'

A sardonic smile touched the hard mouth. 'I was with him in the ambulance. He asked me to find you and bring you back.'

She swallowed on a tight throat. 'I don't believe it!'

'That's up to you,' he drawled, 'but it makes no difference. You're coming home tonight if I have to drag you every step of the way.'

Vicky stood up, dizzy, staring down at his black head. 'Then you'll just have to drag me!' she said fiercely. 'I know my own father better than you do. I'm his only child! And I'm telling you now that he hates my guts!' Hot tears burnt her eyes. 'He always has!'

Scott's mouth tightened. 'He might be dying. Don't you care?'

Stung, she said furiously, 'Of course I care!' She looked at him, helpless to communicate the depth of her fear at the thought of going back there. 'But *he* doesn't. He never did. He used to——' She broke off, her mouth bitter. 'Oh, what's the point? You're not a Foxdale. You'd never understand!' She turned her back on him, arms folded, walked across the room, staring at the floor, trying to calm her racing thoughts. Daddy . . . God if only she could believe he wanted to see her. She would run back to Challa in her bare feet if he really did. But she knew him better than that. He'd made it clear enough to her, all through her childhood.

She was no Foxdale. She was the spitting image of her mother, and he hated her mother even more than he hated Vicky.

'Wouldn't I?' Scott was behind her, his voice icy. 'Try me.'

She shook her head, mouth clamped into stubborn, hurt silence.

His hands caught her shoulders, spun her to face him, ignoring her startled gasp. 'I said try me, Vicky,' he bit out. 'I'm not going without you, but

I'm willing to listen if you think there's a good reason for all this.'

Her eyes sought his, burnt with unshed tears, and she burst out, 'Long story! Got a couple of days?'

His mouth hardened. 'Funny. Try again.'

She studied him for a moment, then sighed, dropping her gaze. She ran a hand through her dark hair. 'You remember my mother?'

Scott nodded, eyes narrowed. 'Lizbett. I was very upset when she died.'

Her mouth twisted. 'So was my father!' she said bitterly. 'In fact, he was so upset he hasn't mentioned her name since.'

Scott frowned. 'So I'm given to understand. I never knew why, though. I left—remember? Just before her death.'

'Ah.' Vicky gave him a brittle smile that didn't reach her eyes. 'So you don't know?'

His hands bit into her slim shoulders. 'Stop talking in riddles, Vicky. Put it on the line.'

Vicky studied him for a long moment, then looked away, her voice barely audible as she said, 'My mother died in Michael Sullivan's arms. They were on a train between Milan and Rome. They were in a sleeping compartment when the train veered off the tracks just outside Parma, straight into a forest. When they cut the bodies out, they were naked. They were in bed.' Vicky's voice had grown stronger with each sentence and was now icy cold, as was her skin. 'They were running away together. She'd left my father.'

There was a stunned silence, and Scott stared at her, grey eyes absolutely still. Vicky looked at him, mouth trembling and said huskily, 'He never forgave her, even though she was dead.' She moved away and his hands fell, dropping to his sides as he watched her slender body, saw the tension in her shoulders, her back, her waist, saw the way she bent her head, vulnerable and very, very young. 'He put all her pictures in the attic,' Vicky continued huskily. 'He removed every last trace of her from the house. I wasn't allowed to mention her. If and when I did, I was sent to my room, locked in and not allowed out again until morning.'

Scott watched her, his face very grave. 'I'm sorry,' he said deeply. 'I had no idea.'

'You must have heard something,' she said angrily, looking over one slim shoulder, 'Challarran is such a small town. I know how they gossip.' Her eyes searched his, intent, anxious, fearful. 'Have you . . . heard any gossip about me? Any,' she cleared her throat, 'rumours?'

He studied her silently then gave a brief nod. 'I can't deny it. There is talk.'

Vicky waited, her face white.

He was silent for a moment then came towards her, moved in front of her, slid one hand beneath her chin and pushed it up, looking at the bright, tear-filled eyes. 'But it's all a terribly long time ago now, Vicky. You have to forgive and forget.'

The dark brows rose steeply. 'You have to forgive him while there's still time.'

Vicky looked at that dark, clever face and a tear rolled out over her lashes, down her cheek. 'I can't!' she whispered rawly. 'It hurts too much!'

'More than death?' came the cutting reply, and she caught her breath, staring, speechless. Scott scrutinised her, his face hard. 'Think of him, Vicky. Try to be a little more adult.'

She flushed but could not reply.

'That's what he's up against,' he went on, watching her face. 'Death is very final, Vicky. And, like it or not, you're his daughter. He's the only father you've got. You must go to him or you'll regret it for the rest of your life.'

Vicky couldn't take her eyes off his face, her heartbeat slowly thudding acceptance of what he said. He was right and she knew it. She had to go; she had no other option.

Swallowing, her throat rough with unshed tears, she said, 'I'll go and pack.'

Scott nodded, then released her, stepping back.

Vicky walked unsteadily to the door, then a thought struck her and she turned back, looking at the tall, powerful man dressed in black who had just blown a hole right through the wall she had built around herself.

'How did you get in?' she asked, frowning. 'Did you break a window?'

He gave a soft laugh, showing predatory white teeth. 'No, Vicky,' he drawled. 'I knocked on the front door like any ordinary human being. Your flatmate let me in.'

Her eyes widened. 'Has she gone to bed?' She would be glad of the company, would go and talk to her. She and Josephine often woke each other up in times of crisis and talked till dawn. Vicky desperately needed to talk now, more than she ever had done in her life.

Scott shook his dark head. 'She had a call from her boyfriend,' glancing at his watch, 'at midnight. She went out in a hurry to meet him at some club.'

Vicky's heart sank. 'Tim . . . yes, she often meets him after a gig.'

'I hope he's a better bet than your boyfriend,' Scott drawled with wry inflection.

She flushed angrily and went out, slamming the door. It was rotten luck that Scott should turn up just as Spike turned into a two-headed monster. On the other hand, she thought with a shiver, it was very good luck. Spike had been a lot stronger than she'd thought, and a lot more demanding. How on earth had six months of casual friendship turned into such an ugly scene?

She went into the bedroom, closed the door and leant on it, staring blankly at the absurdly feminine dressing-table in the corner, the lace fan propped to one side, the pearls spilling out on to the glass-topped surface, the jars and bottles of cosmetics, the French perfume, the fat, soft, fluffy make-up brushes bursting in an orgy of colour from their flowered container. Beneath the green-gold drawers, elegant legs stood supporting the dressing-table, and a pair of scarlet patent leather high heels stood beside a jeweller's box with diamonds and sapphires spilling out on black velvet.

Her dressing-table. Her bedroom. The one she should have had as a child, the one with the pretty, adored, long-haired girl smiling in the mirror, the girl she had never been.

On the wall above her white lace bed, Marilyn Monroe smiled down in sympathy, her exquisite white face a breathtaking portrait of masochistic beauty.

Vicky suddenly saw herself reflected in the mirror, saw the smart, sophisticated, sexy young woman with long hair and long legs, and knew her father would turn white with anger at the sight of her.

Tears burnt her eyes. He still had the power to hurt her after all these years. Five years away from that dusty mausoleum of a house, five years away from his threatening dominance.

It hadn't changed one inch. She might just as well have stayed away ten or twenty years, because the problem had not been solved. Just postponed.

She saw that now, through her tears, as she went to the wardrobe and took her clothes out, the clothes her father would hate, and threw them in a small suitcase.

She remembered Scott's words suddenly. 'Think of him, Vicky. Try to be a little more adult.'

Slowly, she sank on to the bed, her face in her hands, and wept. I don't even know my father—how can I possibly put myself in his place? she realised. All she knew was the terrifying black shadow who had haunted her childhood, made her dress in plain, unflattering clothes and scrape her hair back and refused to let her bring home her friends.

As a child, she had been able to bear it. Obedient and terrified, she had done whatever he told her to do, and forced her vibrant, uninhibited personality into the mould he'd insisted she live in. The perfect daughter—at least he had stopped beating her, hounding her, disapproving of her.

Unfortunately, it was only a matter of time before the lie exploded.

At fourteen, her body had blossomed, and suddenly men were staring at her. Openly, in the street, driving their bikes into lamp-posts, tripping over their own feet as their eyes followed her.

Vicky had revelled in it. It was the first sign of love from men she had ever experienced, and she was starving for attention.

The double life had begun. At home, she was plain and good and obedient. Outside . . . she was free. Free to swing her hips and toss her long hair and smile from beneath her lashes at the men who filled the yawning gap in her life as they stared after her and whistled and made her feel adored.

Of course, it had been a collision course with disaster.

She clenched her fists, tears scalding her eyes. It wasn't my fault. I couldn't help it. I had to turn my face to the sunlight, escape the awful, suffocating darkness of Challa.

'Think of him . . .' Scott's voice said in her mind, and suddenly she did. Just for a brief second, only a glimpse, she saw her father, humiliated by his beautiful young wife, and left in the midst of a devastating scandal to bring up his only child: a daughter the exact image of her mother.

Then it was gone, and she was left in her bedroom on the narrow, frivolous white bed, lonely and confused. What about me? Why didn't he ever think about me?

Scott tapped on the door. 'I want to get to Challarran before dawn, Vicky.' The cool voice snapped her out of her reverie. 'Get a move on.'

She sat up, snapped the case shut, stood up. 'Coming!'

He pushed open the door, startling her. She tensed, standing in the centre of the room, the light picking out fiery red in her dark hair.

Scott's grey eyes flickered slowly around the room, taking in the femininity of it all, the lace and pearls and perfume, the soft white carpet, the dark red velvet curtains, the black and white photograph of Monroe, and Vicky in the centre of it, long hair tumbling over slim shoulders, her figure a sensual paradise, with full breasts and tiny waist and softly curved hips.

'Glamorous background,' he drawled softly, sliding his hands in his black trouser pockets, legs apart in a stance of absolute masculine authority that made her tremble as he looked at her from beneath hooded lids. 'And you're the star.'

Vicky was silent, her eyes wary.

'How many shows a week?' Scott drawled with sardonic malice. 'Or aren't you the kind that tells? Maybe you like your men to——'

'Scott, don't! ' she whispered, face averted, and he broke off, studying her in silence. It was electric. It crackled between them and she felt so overpoweringly aware of his lean, hard body and the sheer masculinity of him that it seemed almost to overbalance her room and her mind, redressing the balance of all that femininity and making something lock into place in her head.

Images exploded into her mind. His red silk tie on her bedroom floor. The hard, driving body forcing her on to the bed, and the grey eyes watching her with ruthless sexual understanding.

It terrified her.

Scott watched her for a second. He must have thought her mad. His face was unreadable, his eyes motionless.

Then he said coolly, 'OK,' and stepped back. 'Let's go.'

Vicky walked towards him without looking up, intensely aware of him and hating herself for it. As she passed him she felt that spark leap between them again and knew a fear so deep that it almost overtook her fear for her father's life.

CHAPTER TWO

FIRE streaked the Cornish sky as they drove into Challarran at dawn. White houses dotted the rich green cliffs, and gulls flew above them, above the blue-white sea and the sleeping town as the black Ferrari sped through deserted streets in the cold dawn light.

The drive down had been so tense . . . Vicky had been aware of that hard body and silent strength all through the night, the darkness somehow making it more intense, sealing them in together in a private force field of strong sexual attraction.

'We're here.' Scott turned into the car park, and Vicky looked at the grey stone building, shivering.

He walked ahead of her across the forecourt, opened the double door for her, watched her walk through, and as her body brushed his she felt that spark leap between them again. Her mouth went dry.

She followed him along shiny white corridors, past wards that were neat, disciplined, hushed. Intensive care loomed ahead. Vicky walked in after Scott. A nurse came towards them. Scott spoke in a cool, deep voice. Vicky studied the doors to her father's room in panic. Then they were being led through, and there was no more time to think.

The first thing that struck her was how ordinary

27

he looked. Just an old man lying propped against pillows in a hospital bed.

Then James Foxdale looked up from that white bed, and his icy blue eyes were still as fierce.

'Mustn't tire him . . .' the nurse was whispering, but Vicky barely heard. She was staring at her father through her dark lashes, seeing how much older he'd grown, the leonine head now completely silver, his brows silver arches and the bones beneath his lined skin making him look even more autocratic. Five years had changed him, hardened him—but the heart attack had been a blow. She'd never seen him look as human as he did today. Never seen him vulnerable. He lay in bed, pale blue pyjama jacket loose on his chest.

Vicky gathered all her courage in one hand and walked slowly over to the bed.

'Hello, Daddy . . .' she said huskily.

The blue eyes flickered over her. 'Scott found you, then . . .' His voice was throaty. 'Where? In London?'

She nodded, alarmed by the quiet voice. He had always been so commanding, so authoritative, his voice enough to stop her like a whiplash and make her obedient.

'I thought you'd go there,' James said, nodding. 'At the centre of things . . . fashion . . . the theatre . . . it was your mother's favourite city.'

Her mother! Vicky stared. He had mentioned her. The silence rang in her ears and she said quickly, huskily, 'Someone told me she lived there once . . .'

'In Chelsea,' her father agreed, coughing weakly, frowning. 'Her parents lived there all their lives.'

She didn't dare speak.

After a moment, the blue eyes flickered austerely over her. 'Scarlet . . .' he said, eyeing her coat. 'It was her favourite colour.'

Slowly, Vicky sank on to the chair beside the bed. 'People say she was very beautiful. I wish I'd known her better.'

The morning light flashed on his silver hair as he turned his head. 'She was very like you. You only need look in the mirror.'

There was a lump in her throat. 'I remember a painting of her,' she said hesitantly. 'It used to hang in the drawing-room . . .'

'It's in the attic,' James told her coolly, then said, 'Are you planning to stay long? Or is this just a fleeting visit?'

Surprised, she said, 'Oh, I'm planning to stay at Challa, of course. Until you're well enough to come home.'

He looked away immediately, his face tight, but for a second she would have sworn she saw the fierce sheen of tears in his blue eyes. 'I'm sure you'll find Challa very comfortable. Mrs Wendle is still my housekeeper, and of course you'll have Scott to keep you company.'

'Scott?' Vicky stared, then turned her head to look behind her where Scott stood, dark and broad-shouldered and silent, at the back of the room.

His grey eyes met hers, and the tough, cynical face gave nothing away.

'But . . .' she turned back, breathless, to her father '. . . there's no need for Scott to stay at Challa.'

'Why not?' James frowned. 'He's been living there for six months, Victoria. And he practically runs Foxdale's for me. I don't know what I'd do without him.'

She stared at him in stunned silence.

'I'm sorry . . .' The nurse was coming forwards now, and Vicky looked up at her, white-faced, suddenly recognising her as the baker's daughter, a girl with pale, wispy blonde hair and a sweet face who reminded her vividly of her childhood in Challarran: of the harbour and the smell of freshly baked bread and gulls crying. 'I'll have to ask you to leave now. Your father needs all the rest he can get.'

'Of course . . .' Vicky stood up shakily, hesitated, then bent and brushed her lips across her father's hard cheekbone in a ghost of a kiss.

Vicky followed Scott out in a daze, standing shell-shocked while he talked to the sister in charge of intensive care, then walked silently beside him to the car and out into the cold autumn morning.

'When did you start working for my father?' she asked him carefully as they drove out of the car park.

Scott looked relaxed, lazy, one arm on the window-sill as he drove, wind whipping his black hair. 'When I came back from New York. Four years ago!'

'What position do you hold in the firm?' she asked, dry-mouthed.

'Senior partner.' He flicked a lazy grey glance at her, smiling coolly. 'Officially.' He changed gear with one long brown hand. 'But with James out of action I'm now chairman of the board.'

Vicky was so furious she could barely speak. 'Managing director, then?'

He ran a hand through his hair, smiling coolly. 'Mmm.'

She looked out at the winding town street, struggling not to show how angry she felt. He was Daddy's right-hand man. Not just that, but he obviously ran Foxdale's now from top to bottom.

'What exactly,' she asked with cool politeness, 'did you do in New York?'

'Made my fortune,' he drawled.

Vicky gave a thin smile. 'How?'

He flashed her a charming smile, grey eyes clever. 'Wall Street—how else?'

'How else indeed?' she murmured, running a hand through her dark hair. 'Wasn't your father in finance or something? I seem to remember Daddy mentioning it once . . .'

He gave a cool nod. 'He was managing director of Arkell's for twenty years. Up until his death.'

Not a flicker of emotion registered on that hard face as he spoke, his voice even and cool and expressionless. 'The company's gone downhill ever since, of course. The eldest son took over and . . .' he smiled lazily '. . . just couldn't cut it.'

Vicky studied him, thinking hard. 'How old were you when your father died?'

He blinked, black lashes flickering on hard cheekbones. 'Twenty.' He changed down into fourth coolly, said, 'Foxdale's is quite a major concern now. We have offices in London and New York. I'm trying to talk Far East to James, but he's hesitant to expand too soon.'

'Daddy's always been careful,' she murmured, studying his hard profile as the wind rippled his dark hair. 'Besides, he's not a great traveller. Challa is his home. It's everything to him.'

'It's my home too,' he drawled, flashing her a charming smile that made her want to hit him over the head with something.

'Oh?' she said tightly.

The charm was electrifying. Her heart was beating with a sense of rage and resentment and jealousy and she struggled not to bat an eyelid in the face of his powerful personality.

'Well, of course,' he said lazily. 'I live there now, Vicky.'

The silence was thick with emotion. Vicky said nothing, just stared at him fixedly through dark lashes.

'I like travelling,' Scott said deftly, turning

away, smile fading. 'James allows me full rein with our foreign operations.'

She smiled tightly. 'Is that why you drive such a fast car?'

He laughed. 'I rarely drive abroad.' The sun flashed on his black and silver Rolex watch, the tanned forearm and wrist covered in dark hairs. 'We have a helicopter at Challa now. I take it to the airfield at Bristol.'

She gave a brittle laugh. 'Where you keep the private jet?'

'As a matter of fact,' he said coolly, 'it's a Cessna six-seater.'

Vicky stared, her lips tight with fury. Scott had painted her a picture of Foxdale's and Challa that she could not equate with herself, her father, her family, her home.

A big money-making international company! Run by a big money-making international man, she thought, glaring at him. Scott Thornton had walked into it all four years ago, put a rocket under it and blown it sky-high; she could see that quite clearly, thank you very much. She could also see he intended to protect his interests. Moving into Challa? How dared he? He wasn't a member of the family and he wasn't working for her father: he was working for himself. Scott Thornton, clever as hell, making money and hiring and firing and being very important . . . she hated him.

'There it is,' Scott said suddenly. 'Home.'

Challa came into view, perched on the cliffs like

an eagle's nest, a fourteenth-century monster of a house in weatherbeaten red stone with a square turret and a great arched door and a moat around it that had long since dried up, covered now in weeds and grass and a sprinkling of wild flowers.

Love burst in her like a tidal wave, fierce, possessive love, and as she stared at that inhospitable house she felt the love-hate pull inside her, remembering the grim stone walls and ancient tapestries, the minstrel's gallery and the antiques and oil-paintings of her ancestors—all the history that Challa carried locked in its cold, ancient heart.

She'd expected to hate it when she saw it again. She'd expected to feel lonely and isolated and unloved. But she felt none of that.

What she felt was a fierce determination not to let Scott Thornton get his hands on it. He wanted it. It was written all over his face. Look at his eyes, she thought, my God, just look at them . . . the narrowed, steely determination as he studied Challa through dark lashes, primitive desire glittering in their grey depths.

He already had Foxdale's. He had her father sewn up in his hip pocket. And he had moved into Challa . . . magpie, she thought, hating him, magpie . . . get your hands off my house.

A Range Rover and a Rolls-Royce and a bicycle were parked in the cobbled courtyard outside the front door. Old red stone walls rose up all around them. Straw littered the cobbles. The stables were just round the corner, through the narrow wooden arch.

The front door was opening, and tears pricked Vicky's eyes as Mrs Wendle came out to greet her.

'Wendle!' Vicky said huskily, laughing, and ran to her old nanny/housekeeper, pressing her face into her neck and smelling the familiar violet scent. Mrs Wendle's hair was now completely grey and still pinned in its untidy chignon.

'Darling . . . welcome home . . . oh, heavens, I'm so excited!' Mrs Wendle laughed. 'I knew you'd come, I knew it. Sylvia said no, she's a heartless wretch, but you know Sylvia Foxdale!' Her blue eyes danced with mischief. 'Always was jealous of you. Serves her right; I can't wait to tell her you're home!'

Vicky grinned ruefully. 'Aunt Sylvia always tries to cause trouble . . .'

'How's your father?' Mrs Wendle asked softly, her face serious as she held her at arm's length. 'I've been phoning the hospital non-stop, but nothing reassures like someone who's actually seen him.'

'Well——' Vicky broke off, hearing Scott slam the boot, walk towards her with her case, his presence a threat in itself. 'I . . . I . . . think he's going to be OK.'

'Is her room ready?' Scott asked coolly.

'Yes, sir.' Mrs Wendle stepped back automatically, 'I've put fresh flowers in it, too, just to make it a bit more homely.'

'Thank you,' Vicky said shakily, her eyes black with resentment as they alighted on Scott's broad-shouldered frame moving past her in the doorway. Sir? Sir? What the hell was going on? Mrs Wendle only ever called her father sir!

Scott led the way upstairs. Vicky watched him, tight-lipped. He walked as though he owned Challa already. Striding up the red-carpeted staircase, the portraits of Vicky's ancestors looking down in Tudor costumes, Stuart costume, Regency, Georgian, Victoria . . . who the hell did Scott Thornton think he was?

'Can I get you something to eat?' Mrs Wendle called after Vicky.

'I——' Vicky began.

'Full breakfast, Mrs Wendle,' Scott drawled from the top of the stairs, eyes glinting at Vicky with cool authority, a smile on his hard mouth. 'I have to work today. I'll need some fuel.'

Vicky's mouth tightened. 'Same for me, please!'

Scott watched her as she joined him angrily at the top of the stairs. 'Shouldn't you just go straight to sleep? It's been a long night——'

'No, thank you,' she said briskly, putting her nose in the air, 'I'd like to look around my estate first. I haven't seen the old place for years . . .' She smiled sweetly. 'So many memories! So much family history!'

Scott watched her with lazy amusement. 'I had no idea you were so attached to the place, Vicky,' he drawled, turning and continuing his deliberate, authoritative leading towards her bedroom. 'Here . . .' He pushed her bedroom door open. 'Your room. I hope you'll be comfortable here.'

'I should think I will be,' she said politely, eyes black. 'It is my old bedroom, after all.' She stepped in past him, her face haughty, and smiled as she saw her old room. The four-poster bed with its ancient tapestries in cream, red, blue, gold . . . the vast windows overlooking the bay, the battlements just beyond its ledge, the polished wood floor with the rug thrown carelessly over it, the dressing-table and wardrobe in the corner.

'I'll leave you to settle in.' Scott put her case down beside the bed, thrust his hands in his black trouser-pockets, watched her through veiled lids. 'Breakfast will probably be twenty minutes. Is that long enough?'

Vicky smiled over one shoulder, looking through her lashes and saying lightly, 'Why?' Do I need to make myself look beautiful?'

A smile touched the hard mouth and he drawled, 'You could give your hair a good brush.'

Vicky's smile faded into an expression of outrage and fury. She said nothing, her heartbeat thundering, glaring at him.

'See you downstairs,' Scott drawled, turned on his heel and went out of the room.

Vicky unpacked quickly, aware that she was now running on adrenalin. How long had she been awake? Thirty-six hours? Longer? She wondered why she was able to keep going like this, but she knew her father's heart attack had some bearing on it. It had shocked her to the core.

She changed quickly into blue jeans and a black wrap-over top, silver earrings jangling against her long, dark hair, a silver bangle on her wrist. She looked young and modern and very free.

Daddy had been wonderful at the hospital. Tears pricked her eyes as she thought of what he'd said. Imagine him talking about Mummy like that! She bit her lip, touched. Could it be a sign that the bitterness of the past was finally over?

Vicky sighed, staring out with love at the view of the sea, the white foam splashing up against vicious rocks, the gulls flying above it in the sunlight. Thank God he was alive. She pressed her face against the glass. Thank God . . .

Scott was in the dining-room when she arrived, reading the *Financial Times* and listening to Radio Four and eating scrambled eggs and kidneys.

'Isn't it a pretty day?' Vicky said, walking to the Regency chair opposite him and sitting down, the sun lighting on the chandelier above, glistening on the oil-paintings on the dark walls and the silver on the mahogany side-piece.

The grey eyes slid over her coolly. 'A pretty outfit, too,' he drawled.

Vicky smiled, brows raised. 'Thank you.'

He watched her across the table. 'Do you always show your figure off like that?'

She felt the hot colour sweep her face and

bristled. 'I wasn't aware that I was!'

'Oh?' He sipped his tea calmly, studying her. 'You didn't realise that your breasts look extremely seductive in that top?'

Vicky stared at him, heart thumping, unable to speak for fear she would lose her temper and throw this plate of scrambled eggs at his dark, arrogant head.

'No?' He studied her, a slight smile on his hard mouth, and flicked the paper, brow rising. 'Well, it just goes to show the difference between men and women, doesn't it?'

Vicky stared at him furiously as he bent his head to read. Then, slowly, she forced herself to move, her body like a rusty robot groaning in protest as she buttered some toast and bit into it angrily.

'I might want to go out later,' Vicky told him, trying to keep her tone even and cool. 'Is there a car I can use?'

He looked up. 'You can have the Rolls. The keys are in my room.'

Oh, are they? she thought. She said, 'Which is your room?'

He studied her coolly. 'The one right next to yours.'

Vicky nodded slowly. 'The Oak Room. Did you knows it's where the eldest son usually sleeps?'

He tapped one finger lazily against the arm of his chair. 'Mmm. So I've heard.'

She studied him with cold loathing. 'And the keys are in there, are they?' Carefully, betraying nothing of what she felt inside, she poured herself a cup of hot tea. 'Any particular place I should look?'

'My bedside table,' he drawled, eyeing her, his insolent gaze slipping leisurely to her breasts, and she felt it almost as a touch, her nipples stiffening under that gaze. Heat swept her face as she saw the slight smile tug at his mouth and knew he had seen them harden beneath the thin black top. His grey eyes slid to her angry face and he said casually, 'It's not too cold in here for you, Vicky?'

Rage flashed from her eyes and she said nothing, her face scarlet.

He ran a hand through his hair. 'We'll visit James again tonight, at seven. Please be ready on time. Perhaps dinner afterwards would be a good idea? Let people know you're back in town.'

Vicky said tightly, 'I don't want people to know I'm back in town.'

'Very little you can do about that, I'm afraid. Word will spread faster than butter. You might as well . . .' A smile lit the grey eyes as they strayed to her breasts and he said softly, 'Flaunt the fact. Hmm?'

Her mouth tightened angrily. 'Yes,' she said, hating him, lifting her chin with hauteur. 'Why not?'

'Good.' He folded the paper, brisk and efficient and businesslike. 'I'll book a table at Les Halles.' He stood up, swung his gorgeous black jacket off the back of the chair and shrugged into it. 'Shall we say—eight-thirty?'

'That'll be fine,' Vicky said with casual indifference, sipping her tea.

Scott moved to the door with a slight smile and went out. With fury, Vicky watched him depart, her eyes glaring at the back of his arrogant head.

How dared he move in like this? How dared he speak to her like that, look at her like that? She was so angry that she was almost gibbering with rage, her body coursing with adrenalin, every nerve-ending alive.

For heaven's sake, she told herself, sitting back in her chair, he's only a man. He can't take things just because he wants them.

Dimly, she realised her fury was probably due to exhaustion, lack of sleep—shock, too. She sobered, leaning back in the chair in the silent house and listening to nothing, nothing at all. Challa was a place of silence and sanctuary. Its peace flooded through her now, and she let it, closing her eyes, feeling it wash over her in gentle waves of security.

To hell with Scott Thornton, she thought dreamily. This is my home.

CHAPTER THREE

VICKY was ready to leave by six-thirty. Scott wasn't even back from the office. As she paced up and down in the drawing-room, her eyes strayed constantly to the clock, her mouth tight with irritation. He could dish out orders about punctuality, but he obviously couldn't live up to them himself.

Suddenly, she heard the Ferrari roar up the drive like a Formula One racing car, headlights flashing over the french windows as he parked in the courtyard.

Vicky forced herself not to rush out to the hall and greet him, standing silently in the drawing-room, her arms tightly folded.

She wore a white miniskirt suit, elegant and formal with gold military buttons, her hair freshly washed and her make-up discreet.

'One of your files, Jamieson,' Scott was saying coolly in the hallway, and Vicky frowned, moving to the door to listen. 'Everything you can get on him. On my desk by nine tomorrow morning.'

Vicky's eyes widened. Files? What on earth was going on?

'His involvement with Lady Hertford, sir?' another male voice said.

'Particularly his involvement with Lady

Hertford,' Scott drawled, laughing. 'If she sells her shares to him, I want to know about it.'

Vicky opened the door, her face white with anger, and both men turned to look at her in sudden silence. Vicky looked back at them, mutinous, her chin lifted and her brows haughty.

Scott ran a comprehensive eye over her. 'Ah, Vicky. A perfect opportunity. May I introduce my chief aide, Stuart Jamieson?'

Vicky looked at the other man with open hostility. He was tall and thin and white-faced with black hair. He looked like a priest in a black CIA suit.

'Hi,' she said flatly, rudely.

'Miss Foxdale.' Jamieson smiled politely. 'I've heard so much about you. It's a pleasure to meet you.'

Vicky eyed him coldly, folded her arms. There was an awkward silence.

Scott pursed his mouth. 'You can go,' he said flatly, and Jamieson withdrew, closing the front door behind him without a word.

Scott slid his hands in his trouser pockets. 'You shouldn't have done that. I hadn't concluded our business.'

She gave him a defiant look. 'You could always contact him on the walkie-talkie!'

'What?'

'Well,' her eyes flashed, 'it's all very secret service, isn't it? I mean—I expected him to whip out a pair of dark glasses at any moment, produce a revolver from his inside jacket pocket!'

Turning on her heel, she flounced back into the drawing-room. Scott moved faster than she'd thought he would, and his hand caught her arm bitingly as she crossed the room, turning her to face him with a jerk.

'You ill-mannered little brat!' he said flatly, then pushed the door shut and shoved her hard on to the sofa. 'How dare you behave this way? I ought to put you over my knees and—— '

'You've got a nerve!' she burst out hotly, winded from her heavy landing on the sofa, glaring up at him. 'Who the hell do you think you are? Bringing weirdos into my father's house, demanding secret files, taking over the business, running it as though it were the CIA——'

'The way I run Foxdale's is none of your business!' he said cuttingly. 'And I don't expect you to speak to me as though I were an office boy. Particularly not in front of my staff. Got it?'

'No, I have not got it! I'm the daughter of this house—not some kitchen maid! This is my home, my firm, and I'll behave as I see fit!'

'You'll behave as I tell you to, missy,' he said tightly, bending over her, his strong brown hands placed on either side of her body, close to her thighs, his face suddenly inches from her own and firmly determined. 'Or you will take the consequences. And I can assure you they won't be very pleasant!'

Her mouth tightened. 'You may be filling my

father's place, but I can assure you it's strictly temporary!'

'Well . . .' he drawled, smiling lazily, 'we'll just leave that little decision up to him, shall we? Hmm?'

Her face burnt with temper. She said shakily, 'You think you're pretty hot stuff, don't you?'

He laughed, straightening, running a hand through his dark hair, sliding his hands into his pockets and eyeing her in mocking silence.

'But I'm not taking any orders from you,' she said in a low, angry voice. 'You may have wormed your way into Daddy's affections, but I can see straight through you, and you're not phoneying your way into mine!'

He watched her coolly. 'You, Prodigal Daughter, me, Wicked Usurper?'

'Upstart,' she said flatly, 'is the word that I would have chosen.'

He smiled, but a muscle jerked in his cheek and she could see she'd hit home with that one. 'Presumably you intend to overthrow my tyrannical regime to loud paternal applause.'

'Deafening,' she said, watching him warily as he stood above her, his broad shoulders and dark hair and grey eyes overwhelmingly nerve-racking.

'Any good reason why?' he asked coolly. 'Or do you just hate my guts?'

She raised her head, face haughty. 'I don't think my father would approve of the way you operate. He's always been a gentleman. There's never been

any hint of underhand dealings . . . secret files . . .
shady connections!'

The grey eyes narrowed. 'Sure about that?'

'Yes! I know my father! He ran that company
by the book——'

'So do I,' he drawled. 'My book.'

'A book you no doubt wrote in New York!' she
flung, dark eyes full of contempt. 'One I don't
particularly care to read!'

'I'm sure you don't,' he said bitingly. 'It would
be too realistic for a girl of your sensibilities. Full
of cut-throat businessmen and relatives prepared
to stab you in the back for a slice of the action.'

Her cheeks burnt with fury. 'If you think I'm
going to stand back and let you drag my father's
name into the mud——'

He laughed softly. 'That's rich, coming from
you!'

There was a long, tense silence. Vicky stared at
him, feeling the hot colour sweep her cheeks
betrayingly as her dark, hostile gaze met his.

'All I did was run away from home,' she said
huskily, defensively.

'And the rest,' he drawled maliciously, smiling.

Vicky got up, shaky and vulnerable, and folded
her arms, walking away to the fireplace, staring
into the flames.

'I don't know what you're taking about,' she
said huskily.

He moved, walking slowly behind her until
every hair on the back of her neck prickled with

the effect of his nearness.

'Sure you do,' he said coolly. 'It was a big scandal. People still talk about it. You ran away with a married man and your father threw you out. Perfectly simple. Nothing to hide. It's an open secret, Vicky. Everyone knows.'

She whirled on him, eyes fierce. 'I didn't know he was married!'

Scott watched her in silence, his face sober. 'OK,' he said coolly after a moment, studying her. 'I'm prepared to hear your side of it.'

Vicky swallowed, her throat hurting as she said in a rush, 'I was eighteen. I fell in love with him. I thought he just lived on the wrong side of town; I thought that was why everyone stared when we were seen together. It never occurred to me that he had a wife and two children. He certainly never told me.' She ran her fingers blankly over the carved pale green fireplace, adding, 'Daddy found out and caused a terrible scene. Accused me of being just like Mummy . . .' She laughed huskily. 'It was awful! I couldn't take it, so I just packed my bags and left. Daddy stood in the doorway shouting at me, telling me never to bother coming back——' She broke off, staring at the floor, her mouth pursed.

'So you didn't,' Scott said deeply, watching her. 'You went to London instead.'

Vicky nodded, silent.

Scott leant against the wall, his body lazy and at ease. The silence was good. He watched her for a moment in it, grey eyes thoughtful.

Vicky bent her head. 'I take it you believe me?'

He smiled. 'Why should you lie?'

She looked up through her lashes, feeling unaccountably shy, and her voice was husky as she said, 'Did you book the table at Les Halles?'

The hard mouth curved lazily and he said, 'Yes, I did, you little flirt.' Glancing quickly at his watch, he pushed away from the fireplace and said, 'Give me ten minutes to shower and change. It's nearly seven . . .' Then he was gone, leaving Vicky standing in the drawing-room wondering why he moved through life at such a breakneck pace.

Her father was sitting up in bed, surrounded by flowers and cards and listening to Mozart on his personal stereo, a serious expression on his face as he gave it his full attention.

'Ah . . .' He looked up and saw Vicky and Scott swing into the private room and removed his headphones, smiling. 'There you are! Had a good day?'

'Marvellous,' Vicky said brightly, dropping a kiss on his face as she hovered by the bed. 'I slept until lunchtime then went for a walk around the grounds.'

He smiled. 'Funny, I thought you'd head straight for the attic.'

She looked at him surprise, uncertain what to say.

'I thought you could dig out that old painting of Lizbett.' James put his stereo to one side, not looking at her, a stain of red on his austere cheekbones. 'Scott could rehang it for us . . . in the drawing-room.'

Touched beyond words, Vicky looked at him, through a mist of tears and said huskily, 'Thank you, Daddy.'

He shifted, prickling, and said coolly to Scott, 'Any change on the stock market worth noting?'

Scott reeled off a list of figures and facts, quoting various international names—Hang Seng, Wall Street—while Vicky sat beside her father's bed and felt bored by this talk of high finance.

'Arkell's are going public,' Scott said suddenly, softly, and there was a distinct glitter in his grey eyes as he drawled, 'The city's in an uproar.'

'No!' James leaned forwards, eyes wide.

'Front page *FT* this morning,' Scott drawled, every inch the chairman of the board, his hands in his pockets, the black dinner-suit strikingly handsome on his tall, broad-shouldered figure, his black hair brushing the white collar of his shirt, newly washed and dazzlingly touchable. 'I'm getting as much as possible on it through Jamieson.'

Vicky didn't look at him, examining her nails instead. But she felt his quick, cool glance and she felt the heat sweep her cheeks.

'Try John in London,' James suggested, frowning. 'He must have some inside information.'

'He won't budge,' Scott drawled lazily. 'But the

indiscreet daughter might be persuaded to tell me
a few interesting details. Over dinner at Langan's,
of course!'

'Brilliant!' James laughed, clapping his hands.
'And she's already half in love with you, Scott.
Whizz up to London tomorrow and see what you
can do.'

Vicky listened with irritation. Presumably the
indiscreet daughter in London was blind.

They drove to Les Halles in the centre of town.
It was the most fashionable restaurant in
Challarran and Vicky adored it. Decorated like an
English stately home, it had pale blue walls,
chandeliers, a scattering of beautiful mahogany
tables covered in linen and silver and roses, and
the salon was gracious and warm.

'Mr Thornton,' Elaine Amiel swept up to them,
glittering and imperious and very much the star
hostess, 'how wonderful to see you again. May I
take your coat?'

Scott handed her the black cashmere coat and
white evening scarf. 'How are you, Elaine?'

She fluttered her false lashes. 'Oh, very well.'
Her green gaze slide to Vicky and hostility
prickled between the two women for a second,
Elaine's smile freezing. 'Well, well. Little
Victoria. I heard you were back. It's been five
years, hasn't it?'

Vicky nodded without bothering to smile. 'Yes,'
she said flatly. She and Elaine had never got on.

'How's your poor father? Such a sweet man!'

Elaine talked as they were led to their table, and Vicky felt the stares of the other diners, heard their whispers and knew they were all talking about her. It was such a small town.

'Everybody's staring at me,' she said quietly to Scott as they studied their menus.

He looked up coolly. 'What did you expect? You're big news in Challarran.'

'They don't even know me,' Vicky said, closing her menu with a snap. 'They just know who I am.'

'Is that so bad?' Scott's dark brows rose.

She looked at him through her lashes irritably. 'I can see you don't think it is. But then, I've already noticed how important you like to think you are.'

His face hardened. His grey eyes bored into hers in the cold silence that followed and eventually Vicky flushed and lowered her lashes, murmuring, 'I'm sorry.'

Scott regarded her stonily for a moment. Then he motioned the waiter over with one long, authoritative flick of his hand.

Vicky ordered grilled steak with salad, as did Scott. The wine was Château Lafite served in crystal glasses. Silver gleamed under the lights. Scott talked to her coolly about his life in New York.

'I had an apartment just off Delancey Street when I first arrived,' he was saying, smiling coolly. 'Filthy dump of a place. But the rents were sky-high and I was broke so I had to put up with it.'

'You didn't inherit any money?'

He shook his dark head. 'It was put in trust for me until my thirtieth birthday.'

'So you could just have waited?'

'I didn't want to. I wanted to make my first million long before my thirtieth birthday.'

Vicky laughed, eyes dancing. 'And did you?'

The grey eyes held arrogant triumph. 'Every last nickel.' He lifted the glass to his hard mouth, drank, watched her across the glittering crystal rim, and added softly, 'In fact I made much, much more than that.'

Her face sobered. The ambition was sharper than a steel knife and she could see it in his eyes, his mouth, the way he sat, so self-assured and determined to . . . to win, to be the best; never to fail—above all, never ever to fail.

Watching him closely, she said, 'And when you'd taken Wall Street . . . you came home to take Challarran.'

He smiled lazily. 'It's my home town. I wanted my roots back, I guess.'

'And Challa?' she said softly.

The grey eyes fastened on her and her heart skipped a beat at the deadly expression in them. 'Challa?' he asked coolly, not even blinking.

'Well,' she said, looking through her lashes, 'it's next on the list, isn't it?'

'What list?' he asked softly.

'The Scott Thornton "I want" list,' she said

under her breath, all cards on the table now, leaning towards him, her eyes hostile. 'You think I can't see what's running through your head? You think no one else can see? You're as transparent as a pane of glass!'

'Hell and damnation,' he drawled mockingly, 'and I thought nobody'd noticed.'

Her mouth tightened. 'Why didn't you just go and buy yourself a Challa with all your cleverly made millions, Scott?'

'You can't buy houses like Challa,' he said softly.

Vicky blinked, eyes very black. 'You can't steal them, either.'

Scott studied her for a second in silence, and she could almost hear his mind working, ticking over, figuring out the next move. She suddenly saw him as her opponent across a chessboard, watching her, watching the pieces, thinking long and hard and planning twenty-six moves ahead while she floundered in the shallows, trying to match his expertise.

'Yes,' he said eventually, leaning back, watching her with those flint-like grey eyes, 'well . . . you just let me worry about Challa. Hmm?'

Their eyes warred for a long moment. Then Scott deftly changed the subject and she found herself telling him about her life in London, about Timepiece Music and the bands she'd seen.

When they got home, Vicky slid her scarlet coat off and Scott watched her, his grey eyes running in leisurely insolence over her body, taking in every curve of the white suit, the short skirt, pleated and swinging with every dainty step she took, her long, slim legs on virginal display in the white stockings, gold buttons gleaming on her little figure-hugging jacket.

'I don't believe I told you how sexy you look tonight,' he said softly. 'I particularly like the way that little skirt swings when you walk.'

Vicky flushed, feeling as though he'd said something terribly erotic. 'Thank you,' she stammered hotly.

He laughed under his breath, eyes glittering. 'Some women just don't know how to take a compliment! Goodnight, Vicky. Pleasant dreams . . .' He watched her walk up the stairs, and she felt aware of those grey eyes with every step she took, hating him but refusing to be cowed, lifting her head and squaring her shoulders, face tight as she turned the corner and breathed a sigh of relief, out of sight at last.

Next day, she went up to the attic and found the portrait of her mother behind a row of dusty trunks full of diaries, photographs, jewels, clothes and various other belongings of her mother. Vicky whiled away the afternoon leafing through them, smiling at photographs of the mother she had barely known and finding herself surprised by how ordinary she looked, for all her beauty and legend.

Scott came in at six o'clock, but he was not

alone. Running downstairs in a bright pink minidress with black buttons, Vicky stopped short on the stairs as she heard the voices, the door opening, and then Scott bursting in with a dazzling raven-haired beauty at his side, both of them laughing.

'She's hell on two legs,' Scott was saying as he flung his coat over a chair, adjusting silver cufflinks, his black suit dazzling, red silk tie striking against his dark, tanned face. 'I haven't had a minute's peace since she arrived!'

'Vicky was always an attention-seeker,' Annabel Foxdale said, laughing, green eyes bright. 'I'm surprised she didn't demand a brass band to welcome her ho——!' Her voice broke off as she looked up and saw Vicky, furious and silent on the stairs.

Scott turned his dark head.

Vicky met his eyes with a fierce glare.

'Hello, Vicky,' Scott drawled with mocking amusement. 'You remember your cousin Annabel, don't you?'

Vicky looked into Annabel's catlike green eyes. 'Yes,' she said flatly, 'I remember her.'

Annabel's red mouth twisted. 'How are you, Vicky? How was London?'

Vicky walked down the stairs, mouth tight. 'London was just dandy. I miss it. I wish I were back there.' She opened the drawing-room door and went in, furious with both of them. Annabel was her least favourite cousin. Pretty, clever, adored, successful—she had always tried to knock Vicky, no matter what Vicky did or said to stop her. It was almost as though they were sisters, the rivalry between them so intense it could burn into a rage at the drop of a hat.

'Annabel's having a party at the end of the week.' Scott came into the room behind her, went to the drinks cabinet, picked up a bottle of bourbon. 'She wants to know if you'll come.'

Vicky looked round, arms folded. 'Where is it?'

'Foxdale Hall,' Annabel said lightly, moving to Scott, smiling into his eyes. 'Where else?'

'A family affair?' Vicky asked, feeling prickles of jealousy as Annabel accepted a drink from Scott, her eyes fixed on his.

'Of course,' Annabel murmured, red mouth curving. 'And you'll be guest of honour.'

'You mean I'll be the star turn,' Vicky said savagely.

There was a silence. Scott and Annabel stared at her. She flushed hotly, wishing the ground would open up and swallow her.

'I'm so sorry,' Vicky back-tracked madly, flushing. 'I've had a bad shock . . . I'm not myself . . . please forgive me . . .'

Scott said coolly, 'Annabel understands.'

'Of course I do, Vicky darling,' simpered Annabel, right on cue. 'It was a shock for us all. Poor Uncle James . . . he always seemed so indestructible. It's rather like watching a great oak being felled.'

Tears prickled Vicky's eyes. She nodded jerkily, then said, 'Please excuse me. I have some things to do before we go to the hospital.' She walked to the door, opened it, glanced back at Scott. 'Have you spoken to Mrs Wendle about dinner?'

Scott watched her through his dark lashes. 'I'm afraid I won't be dining here tonight. Annabel and I are eating with her parents. At Foxdale Hall.'

Stunned, Vicky just stared at her beautiful cousin, hating her suddenly more than she ever had, feeling a savage twist of jealousy that astonished her. 'Oh . . . I see . . .'

'Of course, you're welcome to join us . . .' Annabel said politely, but her green eyes made it clear that Vicky was about as welcome as a piranha fish.

'Thank you.' Vicky lifted her chin and smiled tightly. 'But I'm rather tired.'

'We'll see you at the party then, instead.' Annabel smiled, her red mouth curving.

Vicky nodded, and left the room.

Jealousy was a rather undignified emotion, one which she didn't want to feel, and as she went upstairs to her room to take a bath she fought it angrily.

Were they having an affair? Vicky switched on the bath taps, face angry. Would he make love to Annabel tonight, when her parents went to bed and left them alone in the elegant drawing-room with its Georgian walls and fireplace and white furniture?

Vicky got in the bath and closed her eyes against the steam, and a visual image smashed into her mind like a fist. Scott's hard mouth against Annabel's, his arms around her as he pressed her back against a white couch and made her sigh against his throat, moan against that hard, commanding mouth.

Her teeth clamped together. To hell with him. Let him make love to her pretty cousin to his heart's content. What did she care?

CHAPTER FOUR

VICKY saw very little of Scott over the next few days. He worked like a demon, she soon learned, and most nights when they got back from the hospital he either took off in the black Ferrari for the office again, or went to his study—her father's study, damn him—and worked until midnight, taking sandwiches and coffee and leaving Vicky to eat alone in the vast, imposing, terribly formal dining-room.

Tonight was the party night, and Vicky was ready to leave early.

She had taken great care with her appearance. The Foxdale family would be out in full force tonight, and all eyes would be upon her.

She wore a black silk strapless evening gown, a large black sash emphasising her slim waist. Her hair was piled up in sensual disarray on her head, tendrils escaping on to her white throat where a pearl choker gleamed against her skin. It was a dramatic, startling combination. Her lips were very red, her eyes very dark, mascara thick on her long lashes.

Scott arrived back in a whirlwind of helicopter blades and restless energy. She was left breathless as she watched him stride into the house, tugging his tie off, biting out crisp instructions to the men who followed him in their dark suits, briefcases in their hands as Scott ran up the stairs, shouldering out of his jacket, still talking in that curt voice as the sound of his electric razor buzzed from his room.

Vicky waited in the hall for him an hour later, pacing the floor, arms tightly folded.

Suddenly, he was running downstairs, black hair freshly washed, still damp, a red carnation in his lapel, the black evening suit making him look terribly sexy.

Vicky stared as he went to the mirror and ran a careless hand through his hair.

The grey eyes met hers in the mirror. 'I'm late. Sorry. Hectic day in London.'

'I can imagine,' she said coolly. 'Did you wine and dine the indiscreet daughter from Arkell's?'

A smile tugged the hard mouth and he drawled, 'Yes, I did.'

'And was she indiscreet?'

He flashed wicked eyes at her. 'Staggeringly. Shall we go?'

He drove through town in the black Rolls-Royce like a racing driver, changing gear with one strong brown hand, sliding round corners like a professional. Vicky sat beside him, looking out at the town and marvelling that it could be so similar to the way it had always been. The only change she could see was in the shops, their fronts more modern than they had been.

Foxdale Hall glittered in the moonlight, a cool white Georgian manor house with elegant pillars and steps set in acres of rolling Cornish land ten miles from Challarran. A long line of luxury cars were parked along the drive. Music came from the lit ballroom. Vicky could see the well-dressed guests through the long french windows and her nerves tightened.

Heart thudding, she got out of the car and walked beside Scott towards the house. They'd all be there. They were probably talking about her now. Her mouth went dry with panic and she suddenly wanted to turn round and run.

'What's wrong?' Scott shot a sidelong glance at her as she hesitated at the foot of the white steps.

Vicky stared at him, throat tight. Then she said in a rush, 'I'm nervous. I feel as if they're all going to stare.'

'Let them,' he said flatly, watching her. 'It can't last. Tonight you're the star attraction, tomorrow you'll be hot gossip.' He shrugged broad shoulders. 'But in a week, two weeks from now? You'll be old news.'

She smiled. 'Easy for you to say.'

He studied her for a moment. 'There's nothing you can do about it, Vicky. No matter how you play it, you're still going to be seen as racy, glamorous, scandalous.'

She drew an unsteady breath, nodding.

'Just live it,' he said coolly, and held out one

strong brown hand, a smile curving the hard mouth. 'Come on. Give the public what they want.'

Vicky's eyes met his and that spark leapt between them as he pulled her forwards out of her nervousness. Her heart leapt at the sudden physical contact and she walked at his pace, fast and self-assured and head held high as they both swung into the ballroom doorway in Foxdale Hall.

'Scott!' Annabel saw them at once. 'I thought you'd never get here!'

'Hectic day in London,' Scott drawled, brushing a kiss on her upturned mouth.

Vicky looked away angrily, jealousy twisting inside her. Then her Aunt Sylvia and Uncle William were coming over to them.

'Scott!' Uncle William was a less impressive version of James Foxdale, younger by five years and lacking the authority his elder brother had. 'Any news on Arkell's?'

'I'll give you the details later,' Scott said coolly, and the authority in his face silenced William Foxdale.

'Of course, of course,' he blustered, puffing on his cigar. 'Why, Vicky! Wonderful to see you! And how pretty you look . . .' His eyes flickered over Vicky's figure-hugging black dress and she lifted her chin, her face unconsciously regal. 'Doesn't she look lovely, Sylvia?'

Aunt Sylvia swept Vicky with frozen blue eyes.

'She looks like her mother!'

Vicky flushed hotly. Sylvia had always disliked her.

'Come along, Vicky.' Uncle William tactfully took her arm, leading her away. 'Let me introduce you to some people . . .'

The next hour sped by as she was whirled from one group to the other, a polite smile nailed to her face as the questions flew thick and fast.

'How long are you back for?'

'Do you really work in the music business?'

'Of course, I never believed that story was true. Not you and a married man . . .'

Vicky fended them all, even the deliberate insults, with a bright smile, accepting champagne from passing waiters, the cool, clean bubbles soothing her as she kept up her act, pretending the snide remarks didn't bother her.

People were dancing, and as Vicky took refuge behind a white pillar and huge green palm she saw Scott moving against Annabel in dance as the band played 'Moonlight Serenade'.

Her teeth met with a snap. They danced like lovers. They were lovers. She felt her eyes widen and her hand begin to tremble as she stared at them, her mind revolving with the words as her heart thudded with jealousy and she thought, They're lovers, they're lovers . . .

'Hi, Nurse Jellybean!' a voice drawled in her ear.

She spun, staring. 'Charles!'

'No, I'm Dr Egg Custard—remember?' Charles said, looking as impossibly handsome and pampered as ever, his blond hair shining under the lights from the chandeliers, his blue eyes vivid and charming.

'Oh, God!' She was overjoyed to see him. 'I haven't seen you for so long! Charles how are you? How's Emma?'

'Boringly married,' Charles sighed, 'with an obnoxious infant.'

'And you?' Her eyes shot over his blond head, for which the white dinner-jacket was a perfect foil. 'Are you married?'

'*Moi*?' he laughed, eyes dancing. 'Please!'

Vicky grinned, sipped her champagne, then saw Scott laughing at something Annabel whispered to him. Her mouth tightened.

'I expect you've been getting it in the neck.' Charles was suddenly serious, studying her angry face. 'The family can be so bitchy, can't they?'

Vicky sighed heavily. 'They're just curious, I suppose.'

He nodded. 'Just ride the storm, Vicky. It won't last. They'll get bored and talk about something else pretty soon.'

Vicky's eyes slid to Scott's dark head across the dance floor. 'That's what Scott said.'

Charles studied her for a moment. 'What do you think of him?'

'Scott?' Her eyes were hostile on his powerful,

charismatic figure, hating him and the way everyone in the family ran around after him as though he were God. 'I think he's very ambitious.'

A slow smile flickered on Charles's handsome face. 'What are you doing on Saturday, Vicky?'

'Saturday?' She turned, startled. 'I . . . well . . . I haven't really made any plans yet . . .'

'Great. I've promised Emma I'd take her horrible offspring to Lizard Castle for the day. Would you come along? I really can't face it alone!'

Vicky smiled, delighted at the prospect of escaping Scott's authority. 'I'd love to!'

'I'll pick you up at ten in the morning. It's two hours' drive, and Justin will be impossible all the way. Perhaps we could put him in a cat basket?'

Later, she found herself dancing with Charles as the lights dimmed and the band played 'Fever'.

Across his shoulder she met a pair of grey eyes and her heart missed a beat. He was watching her as though angry with her, and she frowned, seeing the hard mouth tighten as the grey eyes narrowed, flicked to Charles, then away again.

He obviously didn't like Charles. Oh, goodie, she thought, smiling at him through her lashes. I shall see as much of Charles as possible, in that case.

Sleepily, deliberately, she laid her head on Charles's shoulder and clung to him, watching Scott's hard face through partly open lids.

They left after midnight, and Vicky trailed along behind Scott on the lawn, holding her evening shoes in one hand, hiccupping gently.

'I didn't know you got on so well with your cousin Charles,' Scott said casually, doing his best not to comment on her resplendently tipsy behaviour.

'We grew up together,' she said, humming a love-song under her breath.

'You were close?' he asked coolly.

'Very.' She smiled through her lashes teasingly. 'We used to play Doctors and Nurses.'

His face sobered, grey eyes piercing as he said softly, 'Did you?'

Vicky said quickly, 'And his sister Emma, of course. We were all friends.'

'I thought you said you had a deprived childhood,' he drawled with cool mockery. 'Poor little Vicky, no friends, no fun . . . wasn't that the picture?'

She flushed, eyes narrowing. 'I never said that.'

He laughed. 'You implied it.'

'Implication,' she said carefully, 'is not the same as statement.' That didn't sound quite right. She frowned, counting the words on her fingers, her feet cold on the damp grass.

Scott halted a few feet away, turned back, grey eyes skimming her. 'You're drunk,' he said in the darkness.

Vicky nodded. 'Definitely.'

'You'd better not throw up in the Rolls.'

'What a disgusting thing to say!' Vicky wrinkled her nose with distaste. 'And you're only saying it because you don't like Charles.'

Scott stopped walking again. She almost bumped into him, her nose against his broad chest.

There was a little silence. Slowly, she looked up into the dark, angular face. His black hair blew softly against his collar.

'What makes you think I don't like Charles?' he asked softly.

Her heart skipped a beat. 'You gave me filthy looks when I was dancing with him,' she said huskily.

He nodded, eyeing her. 'I won't deny it. We're not friends. The question is—do you know why?'

Vicky watched him through her lashes. 'Because he's better-looking than you are?'

His mouth tightened, eyes narrowing on her flushed face. 'Try again.'

'Because . . .' her pulses skipped and she said softly, 'he's younger than you?'

His hand caught her wrist and he said under his breath, 'You're asking for a slap; you know that, don't you?'

'Do tell!' Vicky flounced.

He pulled her very close and she caught her breath, swaying, barefoot and very beautiful in the moonlight, her hair coming loose from its pins and tumbling in sensual disarray around her bare shoulders.

Scott's eyes narrowed and he slowly ran a hand

through her hair, saying, 'Someone ought to take you in hand, Miss Victoria Foxdale. Before you get yourself in real trouble.'

Her heart was going crazy. 'And I suppose you're the man for the job, Mr Scott Thornton?'

A sardonic smile touched the hard mouth. 'I'd certainly enjoy teaching you how to behave.'

She flushed, suddenly breathless. 'Oh, well . . . never mind . . . failed the interview at the first fence.'

'Did I?' His eyes slid to her mouth and she shivered, overpoweringly aware of him leaning against the Rolls, holding her against his hard body in the moonlight on such a perfect autumn night. 'What a pity. Irresistible images were flickering through my head.'

'Such as?' she asked, unable to stop herself.

His face grew serious, frightening, intense. 'Want me to show you?'

Her heart skipped at beat. 'No, thanks,' she said huskily, pulling away, but he refused to let her go, and she fell against his chest again, pulses skipping, staring in dazed hunger at his tanned throat, wanting suddenly to press her mouth against it, run her fingers through his hair. 'I'm very drunk!' she said on a hoarse whisper, suddenly alarmed, lifting her head, dizzy, scared. 'I want to go home. Take me home . . .'

From the house they heard laughter, and Scott tensed, looking round as some guests left, walking along the drive towards them.

'You're right,' he said coolly, taking the keys from his pocket. 'We ought to go.'

Vicky almost collapsed with relief, leaning against him as he opened the door for her and put her into the luxurious car, where she breathed deeply in silence for a second while he went round to his side, amazed at the narrow escape she'd had. Narrow escape from what? She closed her eyes, remembered the way he'd looked at her, and hoped it was only because she was drunk that she'd felt such fireflies of response.

'Be careful what you say to Charles,' Scott said as he reversed out of the drive a moment later. 'He doesn't like me any more than I like him.'

'OK,' she said vaguely, nodding.

He flicked cool grey eyes to her. He said nothing. He probably knows I'm too drunk to take anything in, Vicky thought, and she relaxed as a silence fell between them that for once was not riddled with sexual tension.

She barely saw him over the next three days. The helicopter came and went, she drove herself to the hospital to visit her father, rather frightened by the Rolls-Royce at first and feeling awfully small behind its very masculine, powerful wheel.

The portrait of her mother remained unhung in the dining-room, propped against a wall. Vicky almost went mad with boredom and wished she got on better with Annabel, who could certainly have filled her time pleasantly with shopping expeditions and coffee mornings had they been friends.

When Saturday dawned she was up early, looking forward to her day out.

Scott was in the dining-room at eight, reading the *Financial Times*, a vast plate of scrambled eggs, kidneys, mushrooms and grilled tomatoes in front of him. He raised his black head as she came in.

'Good morning.' The grey eyes slid restlessly over her figure, lingering on her slim waist, defined so well in the black miniskirt, soft white angora sweater and long black suede boots with flat heels. She looked like a fresh-faced teenager. 'That's a rather sexy outfit. Is it for me?'

She flushed irritably. 'No, it's not.' Sitting down opposite him in the quiet, ordered, mahogany-lined room, she said, 'As a matter of fact, it's supposed to be practical.'

'Practical?' He laughed wryly, brows rising. 'Why? Does it all peel off rather easily?'

Vicky looked at him angrily, dark eyes sparkling. 'Is your mind constantly running along the same groove?'

'It is when sexy young women wander into the room in thigh-high boots,' he drawled, grey eyes half hidden by black lashes, and she felt a prickle of awareness lift the hair at the back of her neck.

She slammed the lid on the scrambled eggs. 'They're not thigh-high!'

Scott lowered his newspaper and studied them

pointedly.

Vicky shifted, uncomfortable. She tugged at her skirt to try and look more respectable, aware of his grey eyes, her pulses skipping.

He laughed softly. 'I wish my secretary would get a pair of them.'

'Poor girl!' Vicky spooned a tomato on to her plate. 'Does she have to fight you off all day?'

'No,' he drawled, 'she usually succumbs by midday.

Vicky flushed. 'And how does Annabel feel about that?'

'Feel?' He frowned. 'Why should she feel anything?'

'I thought she was your girlfriend?' She stared at him, amazed he could be so casually dismissive.

'She's a friend,' he said coolly, studying her.

'A girlfriend,' Vicky said, brows raised.

A smile curved the hard mouth. He looked gorgeous, leaning back in the chair, a pale blue silk shirt worn casually, grey trousers loose on his long legs. He was at once terribly dignified and hair-raisingly sexy, as though he were watching a slave-girl from the Chanel advertisement strip slowly for him.

'Not jealous, Vicky?' he asked softly.

She flushed, prickling, her brows up and her face arrogant. 'Don't flatter yourself!'

'Well, now,' he drawled, smiling lazily, 'you might be without realising it. You never know.'

She gave him a look that could have killed ten strong man-eating tigers. Biting into her toast in silence, she hoped the conversation about his relationship with Annabel was over. She also started to picture his secretary, succumbing by midday, and felt a wave of anger with him so strong it almost knocked her off her chair. Arrogant, conceited man. Who did he think he was? In her mind, the secretary was impossibly cool and glamorous and sexy. She gritted her teeth and tried not to think about her, but she obstinately danced in front of her mind's eye in thigh-high boots, tempting Scott while he leant back, feet up on her father's desk, watching her with wicked, grey eyes.

'So,' Scott drawled, sipping coffee, 'where are you off to today in your practical thigh-high boots?'

'I'm going to Devon for the day with Charles,' she said flatly, glad of the opportunity to get him back.

There was silence. Scott watched her, his face suddenly hard, his mouth an angry line. 'I thought I asked you not to get involved with him while you were here.'

Vicky stared at him. 'You did no such thing! And even if you had I wouldn't have taken any notice. He's my cousin. We——'

'Yes, I know,' he said flatly, 'you were bosom buddies from the cradle. We went into all that while you were swaying drunkenly on the lawns of Foxdale Hall!'

Her eyes sparkled angrily. 'There's no need to be insulting!'

'How close are you?' he asked, grey eyes hard.

'Close enough to warrant the occasional day out in Devon!' she said, mouth tight. 'What's the matter with you? Why shouldn't I see him?'

He studied her angrily. 'Because I asked you not to.'

She stared, breathless at his conceit, then started to laugh angrily.' Oh, well, that's all there is to say then, isn't it? You said I shouldn't, so I jolly well shouldn't.'

He watched her in brooding silence, shoulders tense.

'I'll start tugging my forelock every time I see you,' she said recklessly, impudently. 'Or I could always stand outside every time you come home from work and bow—how does that grab you?'

'It would make a nice change,' he said tightly, 'from your adolescent impertinence.'

Vicky sucked her breath in, staring. 'What?'

'Oh, I'm so sorry,' he drawled cuttingly, 'didn't you realise that was how it came across? Remind me to give you a lesson in adult behaviour some time!'

'Oh?' she snapped furiously. 'And what would that be? Putting me over your knee? Yes, we know all about your kinky tastes, Scott. If that's what being an adult is all about, I think I'll stay in the playpen.'

'I believe,' he said coolly, watching her, 'you've already made that decision.'

There was a little silence. Vicky's eyes warred with his, but she felt the hot flush burn her cheeks, and hated the way he was watching her, sexual appraisal implicit in every flicker of the grey eyes as they travelled over her body, underlining exactly what would happen if she ever stepped out of the playpen, and found herself face to face with a man like him. Every hair on the back of her neck rose in electric response to that look. She felt her heart skip two beats. It was difficult to swallow suddenly, and her throat was dry as ashes. She hated him for it, hated him for pointing out quite how young she was.

'Charles will be here soon,' she said shakily, getting to her feet, her breakfast uneaten, her legs trembling. 'I promised I'd be ready as soon as he arrived. I mustn't let him down.'

He laughed cynically, his eyes hard. 'I'm sure you'll find a way.'

Vicky tensed, hand on the door-handle. 'What do you mean by that?' she demanded angrily, looking over one shoulder.

His slow smile made her pulses skip. 'Do I have to put it in black and white?'

Her mouth tightened. 'Are you saying he'll make a pass at me? Don't be absurd! He's my cousin!'

Scott laughed harshly. 'Does that make him sexless, Vicky?'

She studied him in acute silence, her face burning, then, unable to reply, she went out and slammed the door behind her, hating him violently.

CHAPTER FIVE

'STOP it, you horrible little pest!' Charles bellowed across the parkland as Justin ran after a dog, throwing sticks at it.

Vicky bit her lip, laughing. 'Don't lose your temper, Charles. The dog's more than a match for him.'

The cavalier spaniel was outrunning Justin and his sticks with ease, tongue hanging out, great big brown eyes excited, tail wagging furiously.

'I know,' Charles drawled with a wicked grin, 'but I like shouting at him. It's revenge for what he's done to the back of my car.'

Justin had sat on a chocolate bar on the journey down and left chocolate stuck to the soft grey seats and the back of his trousers. Charles had been furious when they arrived. He was obviously still brooding.

'He's only nine,' Vicky said, smiling, 'and terribly sweet.'

Charles gave her a quick, interested look. 'I didn't know you were the maternal type, Vicky.'

'No . . .' Her eyes followed Justin as he ran full pelt towards the lake. 'Neither did I.'

'Suddenly overtook you, did it?'

'Not at all. I've never really thought about it, to be honest.'

Charles smiled, handsome in the cold sunlight, his blond hair soft on the collar of the beige cashmere coat. 'Uncle James will be over the moon. He's terribly keen to have grandchildren, isn't he?'

'Is he?' Vicky was surprised. 'He's never mentioned it to me.'

Charles did a double take. 'You're kidding!'

She frowned. 'Well . . . why should he?'

'You've been back for a week,' Charles said, 'almost living with Scott. I would have thought——' He broke off, thinking better of it, glancing up at the sun through the skeletal trees that had been stripped bare for winter.

'But I'm not engaged or anything,' Vicky said carefully. 'And certainly not in love. Why should he mention my having children?'

Charles shot her an odd glance. 'Scott hasn't mentioned it?'

Vicky stopped walking. Her eyes were intent as Charles stopped too, looking at her, hands in the pockets of that beautiful camel coat.

'Why,' she asked quietly, 'should Scott Thornton discuss children with me, Charles?'

He was silent, studying his feet uneasily.

She prodded his sleeve. 'Come on. Out with it. You've already gone too far, Charles.' She studied his bent blond head, alarm bells ringing in her mind, and said angrily, 'Or shall I guess?'

He looked up at her. 'Oh, God, I've really put my foot in it, haven't I?'

'Yes.' Her face was serious. 'I'm afraid you have. Now, please—finish what you've started, or I'll have to jump to some very unpleasant conclusions.'

He sighed, ran a hand through his blond hair. 'Well, it's just that . . . I heard Uncle James talking about a year ago. He was with my father at the firm's Christmas party. They were watching Scott make a speech, and Uncle James was saying, "That boy's the son I always dreamed of . . ."'

Vicky sucked her breath in, jealousy and pain and resentment washing over her in waves, making her feel at once angry and inferior, as though she ought to have been strong enough to be the son he'd always dreamed of.

'My father was talking about you,' Charles continued huskily, 'saying how beautiful you were . . . what a pity it was James had argued with you . . .'

Vicky smiled, eyes stinging.

'And it just came out into the open,' Charles said with a light shrug. 'What a good idea it would be if you married him and your children lived at Challa with you after Uncle James was dead.'

'Sounds like paradise,' Vicky said tightly, her face white with rage.

'It just grew from there, I think,' Charles was saying, hands pushed deep in his pockets, breath steaming in front of him. 'Everybody knows. Scott Thornton knows for sure. I wouldn't be surprised if they're taking bets at the office to see if he could pull it off!' There was a bitter ring to his voice. 'Of course they wouldn't dare do it in front of me. I'm too high up. Next in line for the job, as they say.'

Vicky was barely listening, her mind racing as she thought of her father telling Scott to find Vicky as he was rushed to hospital in that ambulance. What else had he said? she wondered grimly. What were Scott's real instructions that day?

'Of course,' Charles continued as they walked towards the lake a moment later where Justin was sitting astride a lizard with bright green stone eyes and hitting it with a stick, 'he's already got the company under his belt. Never seen anything like it. He just walked in four years ago and stuck a rocket under it. Blew the place sky-high.'

'He's . . .' Her mouth tightened and she struggled to sound calm, although her heart was thudding with sheer anger '. . . very ambitious.'

Charles gave a brief, harsh laugh. 'Ruthless! Do you know how many heads rolled in that first year?'

Vicky shot him a quick look, frightened. 'Ten?'

'Twenty,' Charles said bitterly, 'and I only kept my place by the skin of my teeth. If I hadn't been a Foxdale I'd have been out like the rest of them.' He began counting on his fingers, 'Dan Walters, Jack Hastings, Philip Carraway, Nick Fencepiece——'

'Nick?' Vicky was appalled. 'But he was Daddy's right-hand man at one stage!'

Charles looked at her, blue eyes wry. 'Vicky,

your father doesn't run that company any more. He just sits back and lets Scott Thornton spill blood from the very lowest ranks, right up to the senior partners.'

She swallowed, her throat dry. 'I can't believe it . . . Nick Fencepiece!' He'd been such a strong force at Foxdale's for so long, his name so familiar to her, even his wife and family people she'd known for years. 'It's so heartless. Poor Nick. What did he do?'

'Moved out of town,' Charles shrugged, 'like the rest of them. You know what it's like in Challarran. If you don't work at Foxdale's you're finished.'

Charles watched her as she walked away from him towards Justin and the stone lizard, the castle towering behind them in grey, crumbling stone, turrets thrusting into a cold sky.

Vicky felt uneasy. Charles's blue eyes were running over her, over the black boots and scarlet coat and the way her hips swung as she walked.

It's just my imagination, she told herself fiercely. It's because of Scott, because of what he said this morning. He's making me feel paranoid because I'm with a man and I expect to be raped.

What had he said? That Charles wasn't sexless just because he was her cousin.

Vicky swallowed, tried not to think about it. It would only keep her as nervous and edgy as she felt now, so it was best to forget it.

Later, as they left Lizard Castle at five, Charles

looked at his watch and then at Vicky. 'I'm hungry. Do you fancy dinner before we head for home?'

Vicky frowned. 'It'll be dark by the time we leave the restaurant . . .'

'It'll be dark anyway,' he shrugged. 'We might as well complete the day. I know a lovely little hotel a few miles from here. The food's terribly good . . .'

They ate in rambling English country house splendour. The vast dining-room was formal and homely at the same time, with severe oil-paintings gazing down from dark wood walls, fresh cut flowers in vases, a roaring fire in the grate, and two neat spinsters taking their orders wearing twinsets and pearls and kind smiles.

Justin, of course, played up throughout the meal. At one point, he flicked a pea across the room with his spoon. Charles kicked him sharply under the table.

They left at ten, after lingering over coffee. As they walked down the white steps, Vicky saw the car and said, horrified, 'Oh, no! You left your lights on!'

Charles ran full-pelt down the steps, wrenched open the door and flicked the lights off. Vicky approached, with Justin dancing at her heels chanting, 'Isn't Charlie stupid! Isn't Charlie stupid?'

'Shut up!' Charles said tightly, getting in and trying to start the car. It made sick, dead noises. Vicky's heart sank. The wind whipped her dark hair around her white face and she shivered in the scarlet coat. The car was absolutely dead.

Charles slammed the door, furious. 'It's not even on a slope.' He glanced around the dark car park. 'And not a hill in sight for miles.'

'What are we going to do?' Vicky said, appalled.

He studied her for a moment, his handsome face lined with irritation. 'We'll have to stay here for the night.'

Vicky stared. 'But we can't! Scott will be furious!'

'That's tough,' Charles said flatly, 'unless he wants to fly out here in his helicopter and pick us up, of course!'

Vicky looked up at the white-fronted hotel, ivy growing up its red-brick walls. At least they were here. At least they weren't stuck in the countryside without even a phone box.

They checked in silently. Vicky watched Charles sign the register, watched the flash of gold keys as they were handed to him.

Scott would hit the roof. He hadn't wanted her to come in the first place, not with Charles, and he'd be beside himself when he found they were staying in a hotel together.

But the battery was flat. It couldn't be helped.

'I'll have to ring him,' she told Charles huskily after they had put Justin to bed.

He nodded, and for a moment she thought she saw a flicker of triumph in the blue eyes. Then it was gone. He was worried, not satisfied, she told herself, watching him.

'Of course,' he said smoothly, opening her bedroom door and pushing it open, lifting his blond head, looking at her. A *frisson* of alarm ran down her spine. There it was again, that sexual awareness. A man, a woman and the pink and gold double bed clearly visible through the open door.

'Goodnight, Charles,' she said huskily, stepping inside.

'Come to my room when you've spoken to him,' Charles said quickly. 'I'm next door. I must know what he says.'

Vicky closed the door with a brief nod. Going to the double bed, she kicked her shoes off, slid her feet on to the bed, flicked on the pink and gold lamp and picked up the telephone. Taking a deep breath, she dialled Challa.

Scott answered on the third ring.

'Hello?' he said curtly.

'Scott? It's me—Vicky . . .'

'Where the hell are you?' his voice sniped at her. 'Do you realise what time it is?'

'We've had a breakdown,' Vicky said huskily, struggling not to be angry with the biting tone of his voice. 'Charles left his lights on while we had dinner. The battery's completely dead——'

'He left his lights on?' Scott said tightly, breathing harshly. 'Do you really expect me to swallow that?'

'Yes,' she said, surprised, 'of course!'

There was a long silence. 'Are you at a garage?'

Vicky wiped damp palms on the receiver. 'No. A hotel.'

This time the silence was electric. She could almost feel the waves of black rage over the telephone.

'Scott?' Her heart missed a beat. 'Are you there?'

'Yes, yes, of course . . .' Scott said very carefully, and she suddenly felt a sharp jolt of fear, seeing his face in her mind, hearing the tight control he was exerting over himself, picturing him leaning against the wall at Challa, dressed in black, his face murderous, the grey eyes flinty as he struggled to pull a mask down over that violent rage. 'I'm still here . . . where is this hotel, Vicky? What's it called?'

She could barely breathe. 'The Grand Hotel,' she said huskily. 'Somewhere north of Dolby. That's the last sign I saw before we arrived.'

'The Grand,' he said, and she was terrified by the cool, clever voice, the dark thickness in its tone, the underlying primitive rage that was being kept on a dangerously tight leash. 'I think I know it. A big Georgian Manor?

'That's the one,' she said lightly, but her voice was brittle and alarm bells were going off in her head.

'OK,' Scott said tensely, 'I'll expect you back some time tomorrow, then?'

She swallowed, her hearth thudding. 'Yes. . .'

'Goodnight.'

The line went dead in her hands. She clutched it, staring into space. Far away, in the fourteenth-century castle, Scott was staring at the telephone with unseeing grey eyes, his dark face filled with barbaric rage.

When she knocked on Charles's door a few minutes later, he was quick to answer it.

'What did he say?'

'He was terrifyingly polite.' Vicky walked in, then noticed Charles had taken off his jacket and tie and shoes. Her skin prickled as she glanced at him; was he just relaxing?

'I ordered some brandy,' Charles closed the door, took her hand, led her to the bed where two glasses of brandy sat on the nightstand. 'Here. It's been quite a day, hasn't it? Brandy always helps.'

Vicky wrinkled her nose. 'I don't like brandy.'

'Don't be silly!' He sat her on the bed, held the glass to her lips.

Vicky looked up at him, alarm bells going off in her head. What should she do? Stay? They were sitting on a double bed together. His tie was off, shirt unbuttoned. Suddenly, she felt very conscious of her boots, the long black suede thigh-high boots that would forever now remind her of Scott Thornton, of his grey eyes on her legs.

'I hope he doesn't think I did it deliberately,' Charles was saying as Vicky drank her brandy, playing for time. 'He's never liked me. Has he mentioned me to you?'

Vicky shook her head. Best to be discreet. 'Not

a word.'

Charles studied her through his lashes. Suddenly, his gaze rested on her legs. Vicky's panic-meter shot up. She shifted, uncomfortable, not meeting his gaze.

'Well,' she said huskily, putting her brandy on the nightstand, 'it's late——'

'I adore those boots, Vicky,' Charles broke in, his voice soft, and suddenly one long finger trailed from the top of her boots to her thigh. 'Did you wear them especially for me?'

Vicky stared at him, flushing angrily. 'No, I did not!' Scott had asked the same question . . . why?

'Come on,' he said, smiling guilelessly at her, 'don't be shy . . . you can tell me. I'd be terribly flattered.' Hot blue eyes flashed to her face as he added deeply, 'I can't believe you're my little cousin, Vicky. My God, I was thunderstruck at the party when I saw you. What a siren! You have turned out so *sexy*, Vicky, you're just——'

She tried to stand up, heart thumping with panic. 'For heaven's sake, Charles!' she burst out, and gasped as he pulled her back down on the bed, falling awkwardly, terrified as she stared up into his face, his body covering hers. 'No! Charles!'

His mouth covered hers and she struggled, panic flaring in her mind. Scott's face was burning into her mind, his grey eyes piercing hers, his hard mouth saying, 'Do I have to put it in black and white?'

Charles slid a hand over her breast.

She wanted to cry.

Scott, she thought wildly as she fought him, outrage in her dark eyes, Scott . . . and she heard again her voice saying so confidently, so indignantly, 'Are you saying he'll make a pass at me? Don't be absurd! He's my cousin!' Tears burnt her eyes as she felt Charles's hand on her thigh, and she heard Scott saying, 'Does that make him sexless?' Oh, God, no, it didn't, it didn't make him sexless, it made him a man who had been aroused unintentionally, just like all the others, just as Scott had told her, and she felt the most violent self-loathing as she fought to stop his hands squeezing her breasts, the civilised relationship they had shared all their lives splintering with each second that passed until it was absolutely destroyed, over, finished.

She hit him. He leapt back, startled. Blood ran over his cheek. The scratch-mark was livid.

Vicky was on her feet, heart pounding with sick panic, running to the door, wrenching it open, her hands slippery with sweat.

'You teasing little bitch!'

She slammed the door on his angry words, hands shaking as she fumbled with her room-key, opened the door, slammed it shut, stood leaning weakly against the door, breathing hard, tears burning her eyes.

Not my cousin . . . not my cousin . . . she was stumbling to the bed, hands over her face, sinking down on to it, crying in great silent gulps. The shock was hitting her fast, attacking her from all sides, and she felt the world narrow darkly on herself, saw herself from outside, hunched on a bed in floods of tears after yet another narrow escape from rape.

It was all true. Everything Scott had said was true. She was a tease without knowing it. She would find herself raped one day.

Nausea hit her in waves. She staggered to the sink and threw up, clinging to the white enamel like an animal as she shuddered.

If only she'd listened to Scott this morning. If only she'd gone back upstairs and changed into something plain and unflattering, scraped her hair back into a ponytail, worn ugly shoes . . .

But how could it only be her clothes? That was absurd. It must be more than that, it must be. Her friends in London wore clothes almost identical to these . . . everyone wore minis at the moment, and Josephine had a pair of suede boots identical to these. None of them ever got pushed across beds, up against walls, trapped in cars . . .

Wild laughter came from her throat. She looked in the mirror and saw herself; dark tangled hair, wild black eyes, a sickly white face drenched in sweat.

'. . . just like her mother . . .'

How many times had she heard that phrase? Vicky calmed down a little, the centre of herself stabilising as she thought about her mother, really thought for the first time, and wondered if she, too, had had this problem, wondered if Daddy had understood or condemned her for it.

Frowning, she walked back to the bed, stripped off her clothes with a preoccupied air, and slipped naked between the soft, heavy blankets and sheets.

If only someone could help her. If only someone could tell her the truth about her mother. Maybe then . . . but no, that was ridiculous. It was what she was, what she was now that counted. Not a shadowy figure of the past.

Vicky turned the light off. She felt terribly alone. If Scott were here, she thought, then caught herself up with a start. Scott? Where did Scott come from?

She stared into the darkness. His face appeared in her mind. Frightening, clever, cool, authoritative, strong: he was all those things and more—and he talked to her, he really talked to her, he said things no one else had ever said, pointed out truths she would rather not listen to.

At first she'd resented him. Resented his cutting words and darts of truth. Now, she realised as she lay in the luxurious bed, she was beginning to want to hear those truths, beginning to want to actually ask him questions in return—and hear those answers, however unacceptable.

But how did he know?

How did Scott know so much about her, when he barely knew her at all? It was all so absurd, so frightening, so unreal. As though he could see straight through her.

Her face flushed hot scarlet as she thought of what he'd say when she told him about tonight. About Charles and that awful, nightmarish scene in the bedroom next door.

Well, she thought, mouth tight with pride, I won't tell him.

She felt deprived at the thought. Even though his words would undoubtedly hurt, she'd be very grateful for them. There was no one else she could talk to about it. Not even Josephine, not really. Josephine was always just sympathetic. She didn't understand the heart of the matter as well as Scott seemed to.

Vicky sighed, staring into the darkness. Don't be a fool, she told herself. Scott isn't a friend. He's not a friend you can count on. He'd just enjoy tearing a strip off you for having induced Charles to near-rape.

She remembered Charles's words in the park earlier today—her father wanted her to marry Scott and have his children at Challa . . .

Her face tightened with hurt pride. Damn both of them! Damn Daddy and damn Scott. Damn Charles, too, she thought, tears burning her eyes.

She felt absolutely friendless, and cried herself to sleep, wishing for the first time in her life that there were someone here with her, someone in this cold, lonely bedroom, someone who understood her and shared her life and would listen if she shook him gently, asked his advice, listened, propped on one elbow to his reply.

But there was no one. So she slept.

The knock on the door woke her. Blinking, she opened her eyes and looked around the still dark bedroom, seeing the unfamiliar pink and gold walls, the paintings on them, the lamp beside her bed. Not Challa, not London . . . the Grand Hotel, somewhere north of Dolby.

Getting out of bed, she realised she was naked. 'One minute!' she muttered at the door as the knock came again, and went into the bathroom to get the white towelling robe hanging on the back of the door for guests' use.

It was Charles. Vicky surveyed him, wide awake now, holding the white wrap close at the throat, the belt tight on her slim waist, the garment voluminous around her slender body.

'What do you want?'

Charles was in a matching white wrap. His feet were bare, his blond hair ruffled.

'To apologise,' he said in the quiet corridor.

Her mouth tightened. 'Apology accepted!'

He put his foot in the door when she tried to slam it in his face. 'Please, Vicky!' He looked distraught. 'I really mean it!'

She studied him warily, dark eyes hostile. 'Can't it wait till morning?'

'It is morning,' Charles said with a wry smile. 'Seven o'clock. I thought I'd catch you before Justin woke . . . it would be horribly embarrassing trying to discuss this with a nine-year-old present.'

Vicky was uncertain. She needed desperately to

believe he meant it. Needed to believe it had all been as ghastly for him as it had been for her.

Slowly, she opened the door. Charles stepped in silently, walked towards the centre of the room, hands thrust deep in the pockets of the white robe.

Vicky closed the door and stayed by it. She wasn't that stupid. She needed an escape route when there was a potential wolf in her room.

'I couldn't sleep,' Charles said quietly.

'No,' she admitted huskily, 'neither could I.'

He nodded. 'It was the wine, of course. At dinner. Then the brandy.' Blue eyes slid to hers, regretful and sad. 'You'll never forgive me, though.' Pale brows rose. 'Will you?'

Vicky sighed, ran a hand through her disarrayed hair. What did he expect her to say? He'd smashed their tentative new friendship to pieces with crude male force.

'I guess——' he began, then broke off as there was a knock on the door.

They froze. Every hair on Vicky's neck prickled. She and Charles stared at each other in silence.

'It must be Justin,' Charles whispered. 'He's too young for this . . . look at us . . . he mustn't find me in here!'

Vicky stared at him, at herself. He was right. Nine years old was far too young to walk in on Uncle Charles and Auntie Vicky, obviously naked beneath bathrobes and standing in the same bedroom. The thought made her shudder.

'I'll hide in here,' Charles whispered, tiptoeing to the bathroom. 'Let him in just for a second, then take him back to his room, just to reassure him everything's all right.'

Vicky nodded, trying to be efficient when she felt confused and upset and very young. The door closed on Charles. Vicky took a deep breath and opened the door.

She almost reeled under the impact of hard grey eyes, a tough, angular face and a firm, uncompromising voice as he said bitingly, 'All right! Where is he?'

CHAPTER SIX

FOR a second, Vicky couldn't speak. She just stared into that dark, commanding face and felt her life flash before her eyes. It was damning. She knew it, knew even as she stared, mouth open, that no matter what she did or said the evidence in her hotel bedroom was overwhelming, and that Scott would never believe she was innocent of any misconduct.

'Where is he, Vicky?' Scott ground out, eyes hard.

'Where's who?' she stammered breathlessly.

His mouth tightened. 'Jack the Ripper. Who do you think?'

'You tell me,' she said loudly, playing for time, hoping Charles would hear and have the sense to lock the bathroom door.

Scott's eyes narrowed. 'Get out of my way!' He pushed past her, striding into the room, glancing around and taking in the rumpled bed, eyes flashing over her, seeing that she was obviously naked beneath the white towelling robe. 'Had a good night?' he asked bitingly.

She flushed hotly, pulling the robe tight at her throat. 'I don't know what you're talking about!'

'Like hell,' he said tightly, and looked

around again. 'Where is he? In the wardrobe? Under the bed?'

Vicky stared at him, unable to speak, but her eyes flicked unconsciously to the bathroom and Scott was quick to follow her guilty gaze.

'Ah,' he said, nodding, 'the bathroom. Of course.' He moved towards it, devastatingly sexy and powerful in black jeans, a black leather jacket, a red scarf.

'No . . .' Vicky said on a low, husky moan, walking shakily towards him to try and stop him, 'you're wrong, Scott, this isn't what it seems . . .'

He ignored her, banging on the bathroom door. 'Come out of there, Foxdale! The game's up! I know you're in there!'

There was a long silence. Vicky felt sick, her hand on Scott's arm, the black leather cool and expensive beneath her fingers. 'Please give me a chance to explain . . .'

He looked at her then, fiercely, his eyes leaping with rage as he said thickly, 'I'm not interested in your explanations, Vicky. Save them for your memoirs.'

Vicky swallowed, trembling, and then they both heard the lock being pulled back, the door opening, and then Charles was revealed in all his damning glory, naked beneath his white bathrobe, long legs hair-roughened, feet bare, face guiltily flushed, blond hair ruffled.

Vicky turned her face away, horrified. The

silence was deafening. She felt physically sick, not daring to even glance at Scott.

Scott slowly flicked icy grey eyes over Charles from head to foot.

'I know this must look damning——' Charles began shakily.

'Shut up,' Scott said under his breath, eyes hard, and then turned his back on them both, walking to the window, black leather jacket gleaming on the broad shoulders.

Vicky swallowed, her mouth dry as ashes.

Suddenly, he turned. 'Sit down,' he said flatly. 'Both of you.'

Vicky stumbled to the bed on shaky legs and sat down. Charles did the same, sitting beside her, and she stared at him in horror. Didn't he realise that action damned them beyond redemption?

'You realise, of course, that this must never get out?' Scott said in a cold, cutting voice. 'That the scandal would destroy you both in Challarran?'

'But nothing happened between——' Vicky began.

'Be quiet,' he said under his breath, mouth a hard white line as those grey eyes silenced her with one icy look. 'We need to get you out of this with a clean slate, not discuss the intimate details of your night together.'

Vicky flushed hotly, bending her head, not daring to speak.

Scott thrust his hands in the pockets of his black

jeans. 'I'll drive Vicky home with me now,' he said under his breath. 'Charles, you'll get the car seen to after breakfast and take Justin. When you get home, you will tell your family that you had the breakdown, called me, and I collected Vicky immediately.'

'They won't believe——' Charles began deeply.

'They'll believe it if you're convincing,' Scott said tightly, his eyes hard. 'And you'd damned well better be, or I'll have your neck on the chopping block.'

Charles looked up angrily. 'Is that a threat, Scott?'

The silence buzzed with sudden dark violence.

Scott regarded him with an unwavering, frightening stare. 'That's a threat,' he said softly.

Charles's mouth tightened and he said in a rush, 'You can't fire me and you know it!'

Scott leant forwards, mouth tight. 'Want to bet?'

The silence crackled between them.

Then Charles was on his feet, red in the face with rage. 'It's my company more than it is yours,' he breathed, shaking, 'I'm a Foxdale. What are you, you bloody——?'

'Get out,' Scott said with soft, blood-curdling menace.

Charles stared at him for a moment, then turned and stormed out of the room, slamming the door behind him, while Vicky sat trembling, her heart thudding like a steamhammer.

Scott straightened, his face hard, and the grey eyes flicked over Vicky with icy contempt. 'Get dressed,' he said under his breath and turned his back on her.

Vicky gathered her clothes up, trembling, and went into the bathroom. The click of the bathroom door was so horribly ordinary that it brought tears to her eyes as she fumbled about, dressing, trying to keep cool.

The black Ferrari shot along the fast lane. Vicky stared out of the window without speaking. Traffic was all around them. The sunlight glinted through skeletal trees.

The silence continued all the way home. Her nerves were in shreds by the time they rounded the corner and she looked up to see Challa rising above the town like a beacon of light, the battlements a windswept red, gulls soaring over it, the sea dancing in blue splendour beyond it.

Her heart reached out to its wild, windswept loneliness and as they drove into the cobbled courtyard she risked a sidelong glance at Scott, terrified of him now.

He jerked the car to a halt, got out, slammed the door and walked into the house. After a moment, she followed him, desperate to make amends, and found him in the drawing-room, holding a glass of whisky in his long-fingered hands.

'Scott . . .?' She went in quietly, heart thudding.

'Go to your room,' he said under his breath without turning. 'I don't want to speak to you at the moment.'

Vicky froze, her face white, then blinked, thinking hard for a few seconds before she quietly tiptoed out and closed the door, tears stinging her eyes as she went upstairs to her bedroom and sat on the bed, mouth trembling.

He wasn't going to believe her, no matter what she said. Vicky dashed her tears away angrily, went into the bathroom and turned the taps on, stripping off her clothes, pouring scented bath gel under the flow of water and watching it bubble.

She lay in the bath studying the tiled walls for a long time. If only the car hadn't broken down like that. None of this would have happened . . . She sighed, eventually getting out of the bath and wrapping a fluffy white towel around herself. It had happened. There was no going back.

'Oh!' Vicky caught her breath when she entered the bedroom.

Scott stood by the bedroom window, his back to her, and her heart leapt at the sight of him.

He turned, and grey eyes slid over her. 'Why did you do it?' he asked deeply.

Trembling, she clutched at her bath towel, overwhelmingly conscious that she was naked, wet and scented beneath it.

'I . . .' she stammered huskily, 'I . . . I didn't, Scott. It was all——'

'Don't lie to me!' he bit out, eyes flaring with rage. 'I saw you! That bed was obviously rumpled, you were both naked in bathrobes and guilty as hell!'

She flinched from his tone, saying, 'But it's not what you think!'

His nostrils flared with rage. 'My God, you little bitch! Do you think I'm blind. I know when a woman has been made love to!'

Tears stung her eyes. 'Well, you obviously are blind,' she flung rawly, 'because Charles did not make love to me, and if the bed was rumpled it was because I had a bad night's sleep!'

He gave a harsh crack of laughter. 'Don't give me that!'

'It's the truth!'

'The hell it is!' He stared at her, eyes silver with rage, then said tightly, carefully, 'All right. If it's the truth, tell me one thing. What was Charles doing in your bedroom at dawn? And why did he hide in the bathroom?'

She flushed hotly, averting her eyes. 'He . . .' She swallowed, embarrassed to have to tell him the real truth. 'He had come to my room to apologise.'

There was silence.

'What for?' Scott asked flatly.

She ran a shaking hand through her hair. 'He tried to seduce me last night.'

Scott watched her, silent and unmoving. The seconds ticked past. She didn't dare look at him, didn't dare face him.

'I went to his room,' Vicky forced herself to say huskily, 'after I called you. He asked me to. He wanted to know what you'd said.'

'I bet he did,' Scott muttered under his breath. Then looked at her, grey eyes unreadable. 'Go on.'

She drew an unsteady breath. 'He was waiting for me. He'd taken off his jacket . . . I . . .' Her voice roughened, faltered, then she forced herself to go on. 'I saw some brandy on his night-table. He asked me if I'd like a drink.'

Scott muttered something unrepeatable under his breath.

'I didn't want to be rude,' she said shakily, 'so I accepted. He sat on the bed. So I did, too.'

'Good God!' Scott was tightly, closing his eyes. Tears pricked her eyes as she watched him, his face hard with rage. When he looked at her suddenly, she blushed, averting her gaze, and Scott said tightly, 'And then he tried to seduce you.'

She nodded, breathing unsteadily.

Scott watched her. 'How?'

She looked up, startled. 'I'm sorry . . .?'

'I asked you how he tried to seduce you,' Scott stated flatly. 'Are you deaf?'

'No!' She stared, breathless. 'I . . . I can't tell you that!'

'You can,' he said grimly.

'But——' she felt naked under that grey gaze, her hand trembling as she held the fluffy bath towel to her breasts '—but that's absurd! Surely it's enough to know that he tried and failed?'

'Not for me,' he said under his breath. 'Not where you're concerned. I want to know how far he went and how far you let him go.'

Her face ran with hot colour. 'It's none of your business!'

'Oh, isn't it?' he said dangerously, and then he was walking towards her, his mouth tight with rage, and she backed, terrified, her heart thudding crazily. 'When did you pull the plug on him, Vicky?' he asked under his breath, catching her bare arm and holding her while she struggled breathlessly. 'When did you tell him seduction wasn't on the menu?'

'Let me go!' she whispered, heart in her mouth.

'Did you play with him for long?' he asked tightly. 'Five minutes? Ten? Did you let him make a fool of himself before you slapped him down?'

'Let me go!' she repeated, frightened now.

He jerked her against him, his face ruthless. 'How fast did his heart beat, Vicky? How fast did yours?'

She stared at him, terrified.

His eyes were ruthless. 'And how fast is it beating now?'

Silent, she struggled. He held her easily, his arms iron bands around her, and he did not have to move a muscle to restrain her, standing watching her pathetic struggles with an implacable face as she gasped and pushed against him, flushing hotly, her heart hammering in her chest.

He watched her. 'You play games with men, don't you, Vicky?'

She stared drowningly into his grey eyes, speechless.

'Would you like to play with me?' he said under his breath.

Helpless, she shook her head, heart hammering.

'No?' he said, mouth hard. 'Pity. Because I'd like to play with you. And I intend to. I want to see just how fast your heart can beat before you start screaming to get away . . .' And then his mouth was on hers, ruthless, insistent, demanding, and she moaned against that pressure, scarcely able to breathe, certainly unable to fight, her body as tiny and helpless as a child's against his masculine strength.

She was on fire for the first time in her life, eyes closed and body pliant as Scott kissed her with a sensuality that almost took the back of her head off with excitement, the hot needles quivering through her body as she breathed unsteadily, her heart thudding as Scott carefully lowered her to the bed and lay beside her.

'Like this, Vicky?' he whispered as his mouth burnt a trail to her throat. 'Is this how you like it?'

She moaned, her hands shaking as they moved to his dark hair, slid into it, and she felt a thrill run through her, overwhelmed by the realisation that she had wanted to do this for a long time, the delicious freedom flooding through her as she touched him, touched his hair, his neck, his strong shoulders.

'We'll undo this, shall we?' he whispered, and his hands flicked the towel-knot open while she moaned, arching as his hand found her bare breast and fondled it, rubbing back and forth over the nipple as hot needles of sexual excitement shot through her and she heard her voice saying roughly, 'Oh, God, Scott . . .' as his mouth fastened over her breast. Her head went back, her mouth parting with fierce pleasure, her heart thudding under his expert hands and mouth.

Then his hand slid along her thigh and she caught her breath, accepting his kiss again as his mouth came back to her, the pressure obliterating every thought from her head as she gave in to her sexuality for the first time and revelled in the sheer sensation.

Suddenly, Scott raised his head, breathing hard, his face flushed and eyes glittering. Vicky opened her eyes, staring at him in surprise, her heart thudding.

He watched her for a moment, then said, 'Who was playing with whom, Vicky?'

She frowned, not understanding.

Scott's hard mouth moved in a smile of cool triumph, and he slowly slid off the bed, straightening, running a hand through his dark hair and looking down at her half-naked body, flushed face and feverish eyes.

'Hadn't you better get dressed?' he said. 'We're

having lunch at Foxdale Hall in an hour.'

Vicky stared at him unable to move, realisation hitting her with painful force, humiliation colouring her face scarlet.

Scott smiled, hands thrust in black jeans pockets. 'You look a little dishevelled,' he drawled softly. 'Or is it frustrated?'

'You bastard . . .' she breathed through white lips, shaking.

He laughed under his breath. 'Not much fun when the boot is on the other foot, is it, Vicky?' He turned on his heel and swung out of the bedroom.

She threw an ornament, a little china doll, at the door and watched it splinter into a hundred pieces, the crash echoing along with Scott's laughter as he retreated to his own room and shut the door.

Tears of rage and humiliation stung her eyes and she curled up like a baby on the bed, hating him so violently that she shook with it.

The drive to Foxdale Hall was a test of nerves. Scott presumably expected her to be vicious to him, or at the very least spiteful.

But Vicky had more self-control than that. She sat tensely beside him, cool and elegant in a red minidress with gold buttons on the cuffs, its smooth line uncluttered, nipped in at the waist, flowing freely over the bust, fitting closely to every curve.

'Not a word about Charles,' Scott warned her as they turned in at the white gates and sped along the drive towards the Georgian Manor, glittering in the bright, cold sunlight. 'And if you're asked, just stick to the story I gave you.'

'That you collected me last night.' Vicky nodded with considerable poise, her face expressionless. 'Of course.'

He threw her a sidelong glance as they pulled up. 'It will mean devastating scandal if you don't.'

'I'm aware of that,' she said flatly, and got out.

Annabel wasn't pleased to see her. Her green eyes flicked over Vicky icily, then moved on to Scott, a smile lighting her lovely face.

'Darling! You do look handsome. I love you in that leather jacket!'

Scott brushed a kiss on her mouth. 'Not too casual?'

'You know Ma and Pa,' Annabel laughed, sliding a hand through his arm. 'Golf on Sunday after lunch—no one's dressed up.' Her eyes fell on Vicky and she smiled. 'Except you, of course, darling. But then, you're always overdressed.'

Vicky's mouth tightened with rage and she had to exert considerable control not to reply. Following Scott and Annabel to the wide blue dining-room, she saw familiar faces and smiled, greeting everyone, eyes dancing.

They had invited a few people Vicky didn't know, and she was introduced politely, aware that their eyes widened when told that she was Vicky Foxdale, and wishing to God she could one day live everything down.

'Would you carve, Scott?' Uncle William offered the vast plate of lamb to him. 'You're head of the family now, by all accounts.'

'Thank you.' Scott stood up coolly, at the head of the table, and the grey eyes slid to Vicky's with mocking triumph.

She wanted to throw her crystal glass of wine at his mocking, arrogant head. Instead, she said coldly, 'Daddy comes out of hospital next week.'

Scott's smile flickered. 'So he does,' he said, carving, knife flashing in the sun. 'To recuperate.'

They ate the vast meal with difficulty, and the housekeeper took various dishes away still half full when they had finished.

'Coffee, Scott?' Aunt Sylvia preened, patting her hair.

'Thank you, Sylvia,' Scott drawled, leaning back in his chair, hands behind his head, smiling arrogantly at Vicky. 'That would be lovely.'

Sylvia and Annabel fought over the coffee-pot. Scott watched them with a smirk. Vicky hated him, and her hands curled on the tablecloth.

A ring at the doorbell made Annabel turn with delight. 'That'll be Lucinda.'

'She's a little late,' Sylvia said, tight-lipped.

'Don't scold, Mummy.' Annabel flounced out in bright red splendour, her dress a perfect foil for all that black hair and those vivid green eyes. 'Something happened to Charles and she couldn't make it . . .'

Scott suddenly uncoiled, his eyes shooting to

Vicky. 'We have to go,' he said quickly, standing. 'Sorry to be so rude, Sylvia, William . . .'

Vicky stared at him, as did everyone else, the silence uncomfortable as they suddenly heard Annabel and her friend walking into the dining-room. The door opened and Vicky's head turned, everything freezing into slow-motion.

A girl stood in the doorway. Her blonde hair was tied back in a black highwayman's bow, her face clean and well-scrubbed and her blue eyes staring in horror at Vicky.

The silence was deafening.

'My God!' Lucinda stared at Vicky, appalled. 'It's her . . . it's her . . . Annabel, how could you do this to me? Don't you know what's happened?'

'What?' Annabel looked from Lucinda to Vicky, perplexed.

Lucinda said, 'She slept with my fiancé last night!'

Nobody moved and nobody spoke. They all just sat there, frozen into an unearthly tableau.

'That's impossible,' Scott said suddenly, his voice so commanding that all heads turned to him. 'Vicky was with me last night.'

Lucinda stepped into the room, trembling. 'Charles told me everything,' she said hoarsely. 'I know what happened!'

There was a little crash as Sylvia dropped her glass. 'Oh, my God . . . I knew this would happen . . . as soon as that little tramp came back to Challarran I told you she'd do something like this!'

'Be quiet!' Scott said bitingly, grey eyes freezing over. 'You're talking about my future wife.'

This time there was an audible gasp from the room. Vicky didn't dare breathe, just stared at Scott like everyone else, her mouth open like a fish gasping for air.

'Wife?' Annabel was white, staring at him, swaying as though about to faint.

'I'm sorry, Annabel,' Scott said deeply, and moved towards her. 'It happened so fast I couldn't tell anyone, let alone you.'

'I don't believe it!' Annabel whispered fiercely through white lips, clutching his shoulder. 'I don't believe it!'

Scott studied her for a moment, then said deeply to everyone in the room, 'Would you excuse us?' Then he was hustling Annabel out of the room, closing the door behind him, leaving Vicky stranded in the lion's den.

Sylvia was the first to react. 'Please wait for Scott in the library,' she said stiffly, her eyes daggers as they met Vicky's. 'I think you will agree that your presence is most unwelcome here at the moment.'

Humiliated, ashen, Vicky got to her feet, unable to meet anyone's eyes, and left the room, trembling, closing her eyes on the fierce tears that threatened to fall if she did not get a grip on herself.

Oh, my God, she thought as she went into the library and felt the tears scald her cheeks. Now what am I going to do?

CHAPTER SEVEN

'YOU must have lost your mind!' Vicky said hoarsely as they drove back across the sunlit winter fields later. 'What on earth possessed you to say it?'

'Someone had to take control,' Scott bit out. His hair was ruffled by the icy wind through the open window. 'You just sat there with your mouth open.'

'I was appalled! Charles didn't tell me he was engaged!'

'I bet he didn't,' Scott drawled tightly. 'I bet he didn't tell you he'd left his lights on, either, but as sure as eggs are eggs I bet he knew!'

Vicky looked at him askance, her eyes wide. There was a long silence. The sun flashed through tall, straight trees on the horizon, a faint white mist clinging to the land.

'Are you saying he planned it?' she asked carefully. 'The breakdown?'

'I didn't think so at the time,' Scott said flatly. 'But in the light of recent events it seems the most obvious explanation.'

'But it doesn't make sense! Why would he want to run his battery flat and have to stay at——' She broke off, her eyes staring at Scott's hard profile as a sardonic smile touched his mouth.

111

'Yes,' he drawled coolly, 'do go on.'

She stared at him, speechless. He met her gaze with cool irony. 'It was deliberate, Vicky. He left his lights on deliberately.'

'He wanted this to happen?' she said huskily. 'But why?'

'I wouldn't want to see inside that convoluted little brain of his,' Scott said tightly, 'but you can be sure his motives were ratlike. He's been after my guts for years, Vicky. Your father was training him to take my job from the minute he left university. When I arrived back from New York and walked straight into the senior partner's chair . . .' He shrugged his broad shoulders. 'It was a kick in the teeth for Charles. I don't think he ever recovered.'

Vicky shook her dark head, appalled. 'But why use me? I can't believe it . . . he was my friend.'

'Not any more,' Scott said flatly.

Her eyes flashed with temper. 'You're only guessing at all this! You could be completely wrong!'

'Oh, really?' he bit out. 'Then why did he tell Lucinda the whole story?'

She lowered her lashes, sighing. 'I . . .' Her voice roughened and she ended huskily, 'I don't know.'

'No,' he drawled. 'Well, I do. He told her because he knows her like the back of his hand. She's a lovely girl, but a little over-emotional, and just the type to go over the top and cause a public scene. Which is exactly, you will agree, what she did.'

Vicky remembered the moment with horror and closed her eyes, shuddering. 'It was awful!'

'Sylvia lapped it up,' Scott said coldly. 'She's been waiting for a chance to stick the knife in since you got home.'

'She never liked me,' Vicky looked out of the window, sighing, 'even as a child. I don't know why . . .'

He was silent for a moment, then said quietly, 'She hated your mother, Vicky. It's not you. You just look too much like her. I don't think Sylvia will ever like you. Just cross her off the list and move on.'

Her mouth compressed. 'You're so inhuman sometimes, Scott.'

He laughed, grey eyes sliding to hers. 'Why? Because I don't let other people get at me? What's the point? They either like you or they don't. Caring about it doesn't change that basic fact.'

Vicky gave a long sigh. 'You're right,' she said huskily. 'I'm sorry.'

They drove for a while in silence. Vicky thought about that awful lunch and wanted to die. It would be all over town by tomorrow. Everyone would know. Including her father. Her heart twisted and she closed her eyes, praying he didn't hear, praying he didn't judge, praying that her life in this town wasn't an absolute washout.

'Don't look so worried,' Scott said coolly beside her. 'I solved it all. It's over. Finished. That story is dead and buried now.'

'How can it be?' she blazed, tears burning her eyes. 'Lucinda is going to tell everyone what Charles told her!'

He shook his dark head, and pointed out, 'The hottest story in town today is our forthcoming marriage, Vicky. That's what they're all going to be talking about, not Charles.'

'Be serious,' she said irritably. 'You know we can't go through with it.'

There was silence. Scott said coolly, 'I've announced it publicly, Vicky. We are going through with it.'

She stared at him. 'Don't be ridiculous!'

'I'm not.' His mouth hardened into a determined line. 'You're not making a fool of me, Vicky. I stepped in to save your pretty neck, and you will marry me if I have to drag you all the way to the altar!'

Vicky couldn't speak for a second, her eyes wide as she sat with her mouth open, heart thudding like crazy.

'And don't look at me like that,' he said tightly. 'I did this strictly for your father, Vicky. Do you have any idea what it would have done to him if he'd been present at that lunch? *Do you*?'

She flinched at the look in those severe grey eyes. 'It wasn't my fault——'

'No,' he ground out, 'nothing ever is.'

'You know it wasn't!' she burst out tearfully. 'I told you what happened with Charles, and it——'

'It was a catalogue of disaster from start to finish!' he bit out. 'Going to his room, sitting on the bed, drinking his bloody brandy ... what's the matter with you? Do you walk about with your brain stuck in your back pocket? Can't you recognise seduction when you're being set up for it?'

Scarlet colour flooded her face. 'He's my cousin!' she said rawly. 'I didn't expect——'

'Yes,' he drawled unpleasantly, 'well, we went into all that the morning you left for a sweet little day out with your ... cousin!' The grey eyes burnt right through her. 'Or have you forgotten that too?'

She felt her mouth tremble. 'I'm not marrying you!' she screamed, beside herself with rage and frustration. 'Do you hear me? I'm not marrying—oh——!'

The car swerved to the side of the road, Scott's feet hard on the brakes, and Vicky cried out, flung back in her seat as he stopped on the empty, silent country road, the hills and fields sweeping out on either side of them in wintry beauty.

'I have publicly announced it, Vicky,' Scott ground out between his teeth, turning to her in the deafening silence. 'And I am not going back on it.'

She was trembling from head to foot, staring at his dark, ruthless face. 'You're mad ... we can't get married ... it's absurd ...'

He jerked her towards him, his face violent. 'You want to be publicly humiliated, do you?'

'No!' she whispered, terrified.

'You want your father to hear all about your night of lust in the Grand Hotel?'

'It wasn't a night of lust!'

'Frustrated lust, then,' he said tightly. 'But who's going to believe that? Your father?' He gave a harsh crack of laughter. 'Think again!'

'I could explain to him,' she whispered. 'Tell him my side of the story.'

'With your record?' he asked bitingly.

Her face flushed hotly. 'That's not fair!'

He laughed harshly. 'Nothing is, darling. And don't tell me you think he won't compare you to your mother, because you know as well as I do that he will.' He studied her for a second, his eyes furious, then released her angrily, his mouth a hard line. 'It's the first thing he'll do, Vicky. The first thing everyone will do. Point a finger and say, Vicky Foxdale—just like her mother.'

Tears burnt her eyes and she blinked them back fiercely, saying roughly, 'He'll never recover . . . I mustn't let him find out . . . oh, God!' She caught her breath, put her face in her hands, tears flowing unchecked through her fingers. 'What am I going to do?'

He watched her for a second, breathing harshly. Then he sighed and moved towards her, studying her bent head. 'Don't cry,' he said deeply. 'I hate seeing women cry.'

'Oh, isn't that just tough?' she flashed, looking up with wet eyes. 'Poor Scott hates to see women cry! Isn't that——'

'Shut up,' he said under his breath, eyes fierce.

She bent her head again, silent, her shoulders shaking with sobs.

Scott ran a hand through his dark hair and said roughly, 'The solution is already there, Vicky. Just accept it.'

Vicky closed her eyes. 'Marriage . . . ?' she whispered.

'It's the only way out. Your father might even have a second heart attack with the shock of that scandal. We can't let him find out. It would bring ruin on the family, and probably take the company under, too, if he died.'

Vicky stared at him, horrified. 'Died?'

'Yes, Vicky, died,' he said flatly. 'It could easily happen. He's weak, he's only just beginning to trust you, and this scandal . . . well, it could blow the whole thing sky-high.'

Vicky stared at him in silence for a long moment, then with a groan of anguish her fingers fumbled for the door-handle and she was stumbling out into the cold air, pulling her coat around her, breathing deeply, the air hurting her lungs as tears blinded her and she stood alone, desperately trying to think.

He was right. The wind lifted her dark hair from the scarlet collar of her coat. Daddy could die if he heard about her and Charles. It would have been bad enough if it had just been the two of them, but with Lucinda involved, and that awful scene back at Foxdale Hall . . . well, Daddy would be appalled.

Another heart attack was possible. Vicky knew she couldn't stand by and let that happen. She also knew that Scott was right. Marrying him was now her only option. She was finally, completely trapped.

Scott got out too now, walking silently round to where she stood, and his heels crunched on the gravel as he came up behind her.

'What are you thinking?' he asked quietly.

She stared at the distant hills. 'That I have no choice.'

'There's always a choice.'

Her head turned, dark and glossy in the sun. 'What? Go back to London? Turn my back on all this forever?'

'A few weeks ago you hated the sight of it all,' he pointed out coolly.

She sighed, lashes sweeping the vulnerable curve of her cheek. 'No,' she said huskily. 'I was just afraid to love it.'

He was silent, studying her averted face. A magpie hopped on to a tree a few yards away and studied them with unblinking eyes.

'And now?'

Vicky shrugged slim shoulders. 'Now I'm not afraid any more.

He laughed softly. 'Simple as that?'

The grey eyes were intent on her face. 'Is this an acceptance, Vicky?'

'Of your——' she met his gaze and said bitterly '—proposal?'

'Hardly a proposal,' he said lazily.

She flushed. 'All right, then,' she said tightly, 'your business deal!'

His eyes narrowed. 'Is it an acceptance or not?'

She looked into those grey eyes and saw her fate reflected in their cool, clever depths. 'Yes.' The word flew softly from her lips in the cold air, and a feeling of *déjà vu* flickered along her spine, raising the hair on the back of her neck, making her shiver.

Scott blinked, then said, 'OK. We'll announce it tonight. At the hospital.'

'If Aunt Sylvia doesn't get there first!' Bitterness rang in her voice as Scott turned and walked back to the car, his black leather jacket gleaming, his face so impossibly handsome that she was suddenly struck dumb, standing at the roadside as he slammed the door to the Ferrari, waiting for her.

Marriage? To Scott Thornton? She must be out of her mind! He would crucify her. All the women around him—her beautiful cousin, the secretary at his office—he would marry her and leave her alone at night while he pursued other women.

Savage jealousy twisted in her heart and she was appalled by it, knocked off balance. She walked to the car on shaky legs as though she could walk away from that awful pain and burning jealousy, but of course it stayed inside her, even as she got in, closed the door and put her seatbelt on with clumsy fingers.

Scott started the car. It roared. They shot away.

'You'll have to stop seeing Annabel,' Vicky stated baldly. What other way could she say it?

'Annabel?' he asked coolly, pretending innocence.

'Yes, Annabel,' Vicky blistered, 'the girl with black hair you've been having an affair with. You remember her surely? You hustled her out of the dining-room at top speed today—don't tell me you've forgotten her already?'

His mouth hardened. 'Don't interfere in my private life, Vicky.'

Her skin ran an angry red and she said tightly, 'If we're going to be married, I am not going to be humiliated by you and that black-haired witch!'

He laughed, sliding an amused, mocking glance at her. 'My God, you almost sound jealous!'

Her brows shot up with icy hauteur. 'Don't flatter yourself. I just refuse to be humiliated by you.'

Scott was silent for a moment, driving intently. Then she said, 'I'll speak to Annabel.'

'You'll end it,' she said flatly.

His mouth hardened. 'Don't give me orders, Vicky.'

'I'm going to be your wife,' she said, hating him. 'What do you expect me to do? Sit back and let you carry on seeing her behind my back?'

'I said, don't give me orders.' The words were softly spoken, and a chill ran down her spine as she looked at him in sudden silence, her heart thumping. He didn't have to speak very loudly to be heard. His face was hard, ruthless, implacable, and he meant what he said.

Vicky shifted in her seat, her mouth dry. 'OK,' she said huskily. 'But you must see I can't condone——'

'I accept that,' he said flatly. 'Change the subject.'

Vicky closed her eyes, tense and uncomfortable while he was in this mood. His authority was almost a tangible force now as it crackled between them, and she knew she did not dare challenge it.

'I . . .' she was suddenly trembling, her voice husky, 'I hope Daddy will be pleased.'

Scott shot her a look of dislike. 'I'm sure he'll be delighted.'

She stared at him. Why had he looked at her like that? 'I . . .' she moistened her lips '. . . Charles told me Daddy had always hoped you and I would marry.'

A thin smile touched his mouth. 'He wants to save Challa, Vicky. It's his life. He thinks that if we marry it'll be in safe hands.'

She swung her head to look at him. 'But it won't be forever, will it? I mean, this marriage won't last that long, surely?'

'Of course it will,' he said flatly, frowning. 'You don't seriously imagine I'm prepared to go through a messy divorce?'

Her mouth parted. 'But I thought——'

'Yes,' he said tightly as they rounded the bend to Challarran, driving into the little town, 'I can see what you thought, and you're wrong. I'm not marrying you unless you're prepared to go all the way.'

'All the way?' She stared at him, her heart thumping. 'You mean . . .' She couldn't say it, her voice suddenly drying in her throat, her pulses skipping wildly as she looked at that dark, powerful face.

They drove through the gates of Challa.

'I mean,' Scott said deeply, 'that you will sleep in my bed and bear my children.'

Vicky started to shake, unable to take her eyes off him as the car sped over the drawbridge, through the archway and into the cobbled courtyard, finally pulling to a standstill beside the Range Rover.

Scott looked at her stricken face, his eyes hard. Then he turned away, drumming long fingers on the steering-wheel.

She couldn't speak, her throat constricted with fear.

'I need a drink,' Scott said under his breath, and got out of the car.

Vicky sat there for a long time, listening to the clock tick on the dashboard, her eyes staring blankly at the courtyard, not seeing the tiny weeds and wild flowers that pushed up through the cracked stones, the weatherbeaten walls with bindweed growing up them towards the windows.

Sleep in his bed and bear his children . . . She turned the words over and over in her mind, unable to believe them until they had been burnt into her without concession.

He had finally taken over—taken the company, the house, and her. Scott Thornton had wanted things all his life, and he had got them, every last one, like a marksman picking off silver ducks in a fairground, waiting patiently, lining up his sights, then picking them off, one by one by one.

Trembling, she got out of the car and went into the house. Scott was in the drawing-room, a glass of whisky in his hands, standing at the fireplace with a proprietorial air, legs apart in that stance of masculine authority that made her prickle with dislike.

Vicky closed the door behind her. There was a long silence. Her heart turned over in her breast as she struggled to find the right words.

'I—I can't do this, Scott,' she said eventually.

He watched her, his eyes hard. 'That's your decision.'

Temper flashed in her. 'You don't understand!'

'I understand perfectly,' he said tightly, drained his whisky glass and slammed it on the mantelpiece. 'You want to marry me to save your neck, but you're not prepared to sacrifice anything in return.'

'That's not true! I said I'd marry you, didn't I?'

'Then I don't see the problem.'

She stared, floundering, then said rawly, 'I can't

sleep with you, Scott. You must know it's impossible.'

'Why?' he asked tightly.

Her face ran with hot colour. 'You know why!'

'I don't,' he said bitingly. 'I think you'd better spell it out.'

She trembled, hating him, then flung bitterly, 'Because I don't want to!'

He laughed. 'Not good enough, Vicky. Try another angle.'

'Why should I sleep with you?' she demanded hotly. 'You don't love me!'

'Don't drag love into this,' he said with a cool sigh, leaning back against the mantelpiece. 'It's so irrelevant.'

Tears burnt her eyes. 'It may be irrelevant to you, but it's not to me. I wanted to marry a man who loved me, whom I loved . . .'

'Then why didn't you?' he asked flatly.

Vicky stared at him for a second, then bent her head, saying huskily, 'I didn't find him.'

'No,' he drawled, 'and you never will, so give it up right now as a bad idea.'

Her eyes were bitter as she looked up at him. 'You're a real bastard!'

A cool smile touched the hard face. 'Thank you, darling.'

She hated him more than ever now. Her mouth was a tight, angry line as she stood in the drawing-room watching him and began to realise that, even if she came up with twenty good reasons why she couldn't go to bed with him, he would knock them all out of the window.

Scott watched her through black lashes. 'Did you really think I'd let you off the hook?'

Vicky said nothing, her face tight with anger.

He walked coolly over to where she stood, and Vicky started to tremble again, looking up quickly, eyes shooting over the hard face, broad shoulders and long legs with restless movements, her heart starting to thud too fast as he stood right up close to her, watching her.

'You're a virgin,' he said deeply, 'aren't you?'

She went crimson and bent her head, silent.

He nodded, studying her, then put a hand on her wrist, pulling her gently towards him. She went, trembling, her hands on his shoulders, feeling unaccountably shy, her heart thudding, unable to look him in the face.

'I won't hurt you,' he said softly, pressing his mouth against her hair.

'Scott . . .' she said, eyes closing, 'I can't do it, please don't insist . . .'

His hand cupped her face. 'What are you afraid of?' he asked softly, and his mouth brushed a light kiss on hers, moving back and forth slowly, making her heart leap as the grey eyes watched her face. 'This? Hmm?' His mouth closed over hers and she felt the fingers of pleasure rush over her body as she kissed him back, her hands curling on his broad shoulders. Her eyes closed as the kiss deepened, and his arms went around her as he groaned under his breath, moving her without her even being aware of it, moving her on to the couch, pushing her back against the cushions, his hands sliding over her body with expert sensuality.

'It's all like this, Vicky,' he whispered against her mouth. 'It just gets better, gets a little more exciting . . .' His hand slid over her breast and she moaned against his mouth, breathless, her heart thudding as she felt those long fingers move back and forth over her hardening nipple, her own hands sliding through his dark hair, shaking as they moved over his strong neck.

The telephone shrilled into the silence. 'Damn!' Scott muttered, lifting his flushed face and glaring at it for a second before snatching it up, saying coldly, 'Scott Thornton?'

Vicky stared, dazed, into his averted profile, her pulses drumming wildly.

'OK, OK.' Scott nodded, his voice curt. 'Stay with it, I'll be there in ten minutes.' He slammed the phone down, looked at Vicky and said coolly, 'I have to go to the office.'

'On a Sunday?' Her heart sank with disappointment.

He smiled, got up, brushed a light kiss on her mouth. 'New developments with Arkell's. I can't miss out on it.'

Vicky watched him stride to the door and open it. 'When will you be back?'

He studied her over one broad shoulder. 'Late. Don't hold dinner for me.'

The door closed and Vicky lay numbly as she heard the front door bang, the Ferrari flare in the courtyard, then the roar of its powerful engine as he shot down the drive.

CHAPTER EIGHT

VICKY met Scott at the hospital after a rushed
telephone call to arrange it. She had been waiting
for ten minutes, pacing up and down the draughty
waiting-room, when the black Ferrari screeched to
a halt outside and Scott came running in.

He caught her hand in his. 'Come on!' And he
hurried her along the corridors, running a hand
through his dark hair, his cheeks flushed, eyes
glittering. Vicky allowed him to pull her along
behind him, watching the back of his dark head
and wondering why he was always moving about
at breakneck speed.

'Scott! Vicky!' James Foxdale looked up, silver
brows raised, blue eyes delighted. 'Wonderful to
see you!' His gaze slid to their tightly clasped
hands. 'Oh . . . what's this?'

Scott threw him a careless, charming smile.
'We're in love,' he said deeply. 'We're getting
married.

Her father stared at them, mouth open.

Scott put his arm around Vicky, cradling her.
'We wanted you to be the first to know. Didn't we,
darling?'

Vicky was scarlet, looking at Scott shyly
through her lashes, murmuring, 'Yes . . . yes . . .'

Scott laughed softly and kissed her, eyes

glittering. He pushed her chin up with one long hand. 'Don't be shy, darling,' he said huskily. 'He had to know sooner or later.'

Vicky looked into the grey eyes and was perplexed to find that even she believed this. It was a though it was true. They were in love; they were getting married. Scott deserved a cluster of Oscars—what a performance.

'Oh, this is wonderful,' James was clasping his hands together, 'wonderful . . .'

'We think so too,' drawled Scott, 'don't we, darling?'

She stared at the hard mouth, curved in that charming, dazzling, gorgeous smile. 'Yes!' she said breathlessly, staring up into his eyes again, thrown off balance.

'When?' James asked, breathless himself now. 'Have you set a date?'

'No——' Vicky began.

'Yes,' Scott overrode her, pressing a warning with his fingers on her waist. 'We want to make it soon. I thought the first of December in the private chapel.'

'Oh, that's perfect,' James said, nodding, watching them with a smile as Vicky pressed her hot face into Scott's broad shoulder, feeling a fool. 'And of course, the reception in the ballroom . . . ?'

'Naturally,' Scott drawled, eyes glittering.

James settled back against his pillows with a sigh, saying, 'Victoria, darling, you've made me so happy. I've longed for this. I thought you'd marry some awful man and refuse to take care of Challa. But . . .' he studied her with love, and his voice deepened, 'you've chosen so well.'

'Thank you, Daddy,' Vicky said, smiling.

'The only man I know who could take on both you and Challa.' James shook his head. 'Thank God I had that heart attack! Everything really does happen for a reason, doesn't it?'

They talked for the rest of the visit about their honeymoon plans, the wedding list, the caterers, and Vicky's head reeled as Scott took control of it all, occasionally glancing at Vicky and saying, 'Is that all right, darling?' to which she just nodded, overwhelmed by his on-the-spot thinking.

When they left the hospital, Scott walked back to his car and she followed him in the cold black night, her breath steaming in front of her.

'Does it have to be so soon?' she asked as he unlocked the car door.

He turned, studied her. 'The wedding? Why not? If we're going ahead with it, we might as well do it quickly.'

'But it's only a month away!'

Scott shrugged. 'How long do you need?'

'But the arrangements——'

'We just discussed all that with your father, Vicky.' he broke in cuttingly. 'Weren't you listening?'

She flushed. 'Of course I was! I just wasn't prepared for it to happen so fast.'

Scott laughed, his face in darkness, only the lights from the hospital building slanting across his dark face to pick out the gleam of his eyes, the cool line of his mouth.

'That's the way it happens,' he drawled. 'Fast. Now, if you'll excuse me, I have to get back to the office.' He got in the car, fired the engine and roared away, leaving Vicky watching his red tail-lights and feeling suddenly achingly alone.

She spent the evening at home. Challa was crushingly silent. Having sat staring at the television for an hour, she felt even more bored, and switched it off, putting some music on instead and settling down to read a book on John F. Kennedy that Scott had left lying around.

When the doorbell rang at eleven, she sat up, frowning, and heard Mrs Wendle go to the front door and open it. Vicky listened for a moment, then Mrs Wendle was tapping on the door of the music-room.

'Come in,' Vicky called gently, curled up in the dark wine-red chair that her father usually sat in, the fire spitting in the grate, the lights low, red velvet curtains falling to the floor. The whole room was decorated in masculine style.

'Sorry to disturb you, Vicky.' Mrs Wendle appeared in the doorway in her housecoat, carrying a cup of cocoa and wearing rollers in her hair. 'I was just off to bed, but Mr Charles is outside and seems terribly upset. Should I let him in?'

Vicky sat up, frowning. 'Did he say what he wanted?'

'Not a word,' Mrs Wendle said. 'He just pleaded with me to find you. He's in a terrible state. Smells of whisky, too.' She nodded disapprovingly.

Vicky thought for a moment. Scott would be furious if she let him in. Her heart skipped a beat and she felt rage and jealousy suddenly prickle inside her. For all she knew, Scott was with Annabel. Her mouth tightened.

'Send him in,' she said to Mrs Wendle.

Charles came in a few moments later, his blond hair dishevelled, face flushed, smelling quite pungently of whisky.

'I hope you didn't drive like that, Mr Charles,' said Mrs Wendle, hovering in the doorway.

Charles shot her a filthy look. 'Vicky!' He turned to her, eyes pleading. 'I must speak to you alone.'

Vicky flicked her gaze to Mrs Wendle and nodded. The housekeeper withdrew silently. Charles waited, hands shoved in the pockets of his immaculate beige suit. When the door closed, he turned to her.

'Is it true?'

Vicky looked at him and said nothing.

He leapt at her and jerked her out of her chair, ignoring her gasp. 'Is it true?'

She stared, stammering, 'What . . .*what* . . .?'

'The engagement,' he said tightly. 'Is it true?'

Vicky nodded, frightened of him suddenly. 'Yes, it's true. We're engaged. We're getting married on December the first. It was all very sudden——'

'I'll bet it was!' he sneered, releasing her with a shove and turning away, running a hand through his hair. 'So sudden, in fact, that you didn't even know about it until lunchtime today.'

The silence was very tense and Vicky studied him in it through her lashes, wishing she hadn't let him come in.

'Am I right?' Charles turned, studying her. 'Did you get engaged at around lunchtime today? At just about the time Lucinda burst into Aunt Sylvia's Sunday lunch and caused that scene?'

Vicky studied him angrily. 'That's none of your business, Charles?'

He laughed openly at her, his blue eyes very angry.

'*You* caused that scene,' she said under her breath. 'Scott says Lucinda's the kind of girl who does that all the time . . .'

'How the hell would he know?' Charles sneered.

'I agree with him,' Vicky said tightly. 'I saw her—remember? I got the full blast of her hysterical nature. In front of my friends and family.' Her mouth was a furious line as she added, 'And you are directly responsible, Charles. How dare you tell her you slept with me? Who the hell do you think you are?'

'I think I'm a Foxdale,' he said, his voice shaking. 'A Foxdale, Vicky. Something you and I have in common. My place is at the head of the firm. My place is here, at Challa.' His mouth twisted in an ugly way. 'Don't you understand what you've done, you stupid little bitch?'

She caught her breath angrily. 'Charles!'

'You've handed it all to him on a plate!' he burst out furiously. 'The firm, Challa, the money—everything! It's all his for the taking. He's finally done it. My God, he's finally done it!' He put a hand to his forehead, groaning while Vicky stared in disbelief. 'When you came home I thought you'd turn to me. I thought we could be friends as we used to be. But you turned to him . . .' His voice shook with jealousy. 'Scott bloody all-powerful Thornton!'

Vicky listened to his words without expression, her heart suddenly hurting although she didn't know why, didn't want to know why. It was true. What he said was true, yet she did not want to hear it.

'He's marrying me to protect the family from——' she began shakily and Charles rounded on her, face furious.

'Don't lie to yourself!' he shouted. 'He's marrying you for this!' He raised his hands, gestured to the walls. 'This, Vicky, this house and everything that comes with it. The firm, the money, the land, the art treasures, the status . . . he's wanted it all along. I never thought he'd get it. It seemed impossible. Not without Foxdale tacked on the end of his name, not without that.' He studied her, blue eyes fierce. 'But you handed it all to him, wrapped up in pretty pink ribbons.'

White, shaking, Vicky just stared at him and couldn't speak. Scott flashed into her mind, confusing her, his face so vivid, his grey eyes fiery and full of ambition, his mouth hard and determined, and his mind clever, very clever, much too clever for her.

She was facing him across the chessboard again, and this time it was checkmate.

Suddenly, the roar of the Ferrari split the dark night, and Vicky and Charles froze, staring at each other in the silent room, only the hiss of the record player filling the silence.

'He mustn't find you here,' Vicky said through bloodless lips, her heart pounding.

Charles squared his shoulders. 'He can go to hell!' he said thickly, and Vicky was afraid, seeing the determined violence in his blue eyes, the need to smash something apart, even if it involved two human beings.

The front door opened and closed. Scott's footsteps went to the drawing-room.

'Please,' Vicky said under her breath, 'he'll come to find me at any moment.'

'How do you propose I leave?' Charles drawled coldly. 'Through the windows?'

'Why not?' she asked tightly. 'You've already proved your character is lacking in common decency. Why shouldn't you turn out to be a cat burglar, too?'

He smiled thinly. She saw a look of sadness in his eyes, then it was gone, and he said flatly, 'You just don't understand, do you Vicky? You look at him, but you don't see him.'

Vicky's mouth tightened. 'I see you, though, Charles. And I know Scott would never have painted me as the scarlet woman you tried to make me.'

He laughed angrily. 'Well, isn't he just the perfect gentleman?' And then he grabbed at her, yanked her, into his arms. She cried out involuntarily, fighting him, terrified as she heard Scott running from the drawing-room, across the hallway while Charles twisted her into his arms, his mouth pressing against hers as she struggled.

'What are you doing?' she moaned against his mouth. 'You fool!'

The door burst open. Scott stood there, breathing harshly, his eyes taking in the scene at once.

Charles raised his head, looked at Scott and smiled. 'Hello, Thornton,' he drawled unpleasantly. 'Just fondling your future wife's breasts.'

The silence was terrifying.

Scott shot across the room, white with rage. His first punch caught Charles on the jaw, his second in the stomach, and his third on the jaw again. Charles staggered back, gasping, a hand to his mouth.

Scott watched him, breathing harshly. 'Are you ready to leave? Or do you want some more?'

Charles looked at him bitterly. 'You think you've got it all, don't you, you bastard?'

Scott's mouth hardened and he said thickly, 'If it's professional jealousy that's bugging you, I think we can work something out.'

'Oh, yeah?' Charles laughed, eyes blazing.

'Yes,' Scott said tightly. 'How does a transfer to the London office grab you?'

'You wouldn't dare,' Charles said hoarsely, staring.

Scott smiled unpleasantly. 'Try me.'

There was a tense silence. Charles got to his feet, eyes murderous. 'I've been in line for your job for years. Transfer me to London and everyone will know you've only done it to get me out of the way.'

'Not if I tell them all exactly what you did,' Scott said in a cold, hard voice.

Charles moistened his lips, eyes narrowing. 'They'd never believe it. I'm a Foxdale. They'd point the finger at you.'

'With Vicky as my new bride?' enquired Scott coolly.

Charles's mouth tightened, and he said on a voice that shook with fury, 'If she marries you, she deserves to lose Challa.'

'She won't be losing Challa,' drawled Scott. 'She'll just be gaining a new master.'

Vicky's eyes closed. Was that how he really saw himself? As her master? As Challa's master, more likely, she thought angrily, looking at him.

'All right,' Charles said under his breath, angry acceptance in his face. 'Marry her and take Challa, and take Foxdale's too. But if I ever have the chance to ruin you I'll take it with both hands.' He turned on his heel, walked across the room, and slammed out of the door.

Vicky stood in appalled silence, listening to him leave the house. Her eyes closed with regret. Poor Charles. Why had he allowed his jealousy to run away with itself?

Scott turned to her, his face hard and unreadable. 'How long had he been here?'

She started, staring at him. 'Ten . . . fifteen minutes . . .'

'You expect me to believe that?'

Her eyes widened. 'I—it's true!'

'You lying little bitch!' he said between his teeth, eyes leaping with rage. 'What did you do—ring him the minute you got back? Tell him I'd be out late and there wasn't a problem if——'

'Ask Mrs Wendle!' she flared, trembling. 'She let him in!'

His eyes flickered over her face; he looked murderous. 'That woman's known you all our life. How do I know she won't lie for you? Don't tell me she didn't hear all that. I should think the whole town heard it!'

Vicky stared at him, tears of frustration and shock suddenly pricking her eyes. 'In other words, you're not going to believe me, no matter what I say or do?'

He looked at her and bit out, 'Why the hell should I? This isn't the first time it's happened! Every time I turn around you're fighting some guy off! God knows, you probably see me as just another contender for the Vicky Foxdale seduction list.'

Vicky caught her breath. 'That's a terrible thing to say!'

'Oh, is it?' he said thickly, his face dark with rage, and suddenly his hands shot out, catching her upper arms, biting into them. 'Well, I disagree, Vicky. In fact. I think it's time you got yourself well and truly seduced. And by someone who knows how to stop you wriggling out of it!' His mouth came down over hers, hard and insistent, wanting to punish, and she struggled angrily, moaning as his mouth ravaged hers. When she tried to hit him, he caught her wrists and pinned her to the wall with one hand, his other hand sliding down from her throat even as she fought him, capturing her breast, hurting her as he pressed it hard. Vicky felt the tears burn her eyes, felt the excitement stir deep inside her as she wriggled, tried to get away from him. She felt his hand at her zip, felt it tugged down, and she moaned against his mouth, breathless now, shaking as those strong hands tugged the dress from her shoulders, leaving her naked to the waist.

'Don't . . . don't!' her voice cried, but her body pleaded the opposite, and as his hands tugged the lacy bra cups down Vicky's moans turned to shudders, and her gasp as his mouth closed over her breast was sexual.

Suddenly, her hands were in his hair, clutching him to her, revelling in the scent and taste of him, her hands shaking as they slid to his strong throat, his shoulders, felt the heartbeat that thudded hard and heavy against her palm as she touched his bronzed chest.

'Ah, Vicky . . .' Scott said thickly, and then she was being lowered to the floor. Scott's body was hard against her, his breathing quickening as his leg slid between hers, and she heard herself moaning as his mouth slid over her breast, one hand on her thigh. The sexual excitement swept over her like hot needles, prickling her scalp, her arms and legs and stomach; her jaw was tight with excitement, every brush of his mouth and hands and dark hair torturingly sensual.

The telephone shrilled into the silence. Scott's dark head jerked up, his face flushed, eyes glittering. Quickly, he reached for it with one long hand and snatched it up, saying tightly, 'Yes?'

Vicky watched him, her hands covering her bare breasts, her dark hair splayed on the floor.

His face slowly turned into a hard angry mask. 'No, there is absolutely no chance whatsoever that you can have a quick work with Vicky. Don't telephone here again. And if I catch you on Challa land, Charles, you will find yourself without kneecaps—do I make myself clear?'

He slammed the telephone down. Vicky watched him in anxious silence.

Face averted, he said, 'That was Charles. Do you have any idea why he might have called?'

'No,' she said shakily, unable to sit up because his lean body was still covering hers.

He turned on her, eyes leaping with rage. 'Like hell!'

She flinched. 'Scott . . .'

'You little bitch!' he said hoarsely, pushing her violently away from him, getting to his feet, his eyes furious as he said, 'You told him, didn't you? you told him the whole damned story!'

She stared, shaking her head.

'Liar!' His voice was as stinging as a whiplash. 'That's why he felt free to make love to you! And that's why he called just now! My God, you're going to make a fool, of me before this even begins!' His mouth shook and he said fiercely, 'Well, I won't have it, Vicky. Either you marry me or you don't. But if you do, let's have one thing clear. I will not tolerate any other men encroaching on my territory!'

'I'm not your territory!' she said, trembling. 'I'm a person. You can't just——'

'You damned well are!' he bit out. 'It's too late to back out of it now. For both of us. I've publicly committed myself to you and I'm not going back on it.'

'I didn't ask you to——' she began shakily.

'And I won't have you telling other people the truth about our marriage! Particularly not that little rodent, Charles Foxdale.'

'I didn't tell him!' She was shaking, dragging her red dress back up over her shoulders and zipping it up. 'He did that deliberately when you came in because he's jealous of you. Don't you understand that? He wanted to make you angry. He wanted to get back at you.'

He laughed harshly. 'Oh, sure—what a neat little story. But not very convincing, Vicky.'

She got to her feet, angry too, her eyes blazing as she said tightly, 'Nor are your reasons for marrying me, Scott!'

There was a short silence. The grey eyes narrowed. 'What the hell are you talking about?'

Her mouth trembled. She didn't want this confrontation, but it was too late to back out now: she'd have to say it all and accept the consequences, no matter how painful.

'I'm talking about Challa,' she said, tears burning her eyes although she kept her cool and lifted her chin. 'I'm talking about my father's company, my father's money and my father's house.'

He watched her, his mouth a hard angry line. 'I see.'

Vicky had expected him to say something more,

and waited, her chin lifted, ready to take that vicious verbal right hook that would tell her Scott only wanted to marry her for her family's money and heritage.

It never came. The silence ticked on, and Scott watched her with those icy, contemptuous grey eyes, his face a dark, primitive mask.

'Is that all you're going to say?' Vicky asked.

'What do you expect me to say?' he drawled tightly. 'That it's all a lie? That I don't just want you for Challa, the money . . .?'

She flushed hotly, studying him through her lashes, the pain knifing into her heart as though he had actually taken a long knife and stabbed her, very slowly, stood back and watched the blood ooze out.

'Then it's true,' she said in a flat, unemotional voice.

His mouth tightened. 'Whatever you feel like believing, Vicky, is all right with me.'

She suddenly couldn't look at him. The pain was too great. She couldn't speak, either. She just stood there, her arms folded, stiff and unmoving, her face white.

He studied her. 'I rang my mother tonight. I felt she ought to be told immediately. She wants to meet you. We'll be having dinner with her tomorrow night.'

'Yes . . .' Vicky heard herself sat stiffly. It was all a sham, then. All for the money. For Scott

Thornton to go through life winning and winning and winning . . .

'I'll be back from work at six. Be ready to leave at seven.'

Vicky nodded jerkily.

He watched her for another moment, then said tightly, 'Goodnight, Vicky.'

The door closed and she stared at it for a long time. The pain just went on and on. This is absurd, she told herself, tears blurring her vision. Why should I feel this hurt?

It was all clear from the start—wasn't it? That Scott wanted Challa, and whatever Scott wanted, Scott got. Of course, she hadn't equated that with this marriage. She had genuinely believed his motives at the time were genuine.

Her mouth tightened into a bitter line. They were genuine all right—genuine ambition blazing a trail across her life.

But she'd thought—hoped—he cared just a little for her. When he'd said, 'You will sleep in my bed and bear my children', a little light of hope had leapt into her, alongside the fear, and she'd started thinking . . .

Oh, what was the use? She pinched herself angrily, glad of the tears that stung her eyes and slid out over her lashes. What did it matter in the end anyway?

She wasn't in love with Scott! How could she be? Look at him! Arrogant, conceited, ambitious . . . tears slid hotly over her white cheeks, ran down to her mouth. He didn't care about her; why should she waste time caring about him?

Vicky sank down into the chair, her face in her hands.

CHAPTER NINE

SCOTT'S mother's house was a shock to Vicky. Her eyes widened as they turned into a vast private driveway with electronic gates and a uniformed guard with an Alsatian. The guard came out of the gatehouse and glanced at the black Ferrari, shining a torch on it.

'That you, Mr Scott?' the man asked, peering at Scott's hard face in the dark, the white torchlight flashing over grey eyes, tough mouth, black hair.

'Hello, Crowsal,' Scott drawled, smiling as he leant out of the car window. 'Is she back from her cocktail party yet?'

'Got back five minutes ago,' Crowsal said, laughing, 'so take your time driving up. I expect she'll be doing her hair.'

Scott laughed. 'While Emmy fixes dinner!'

Crowsal grinned, and went back into the gatehouse. The tall black wrought-iron gages slid apart, and the black Ferrari drove forwards into an elegant tree-lined drive, very French, the trees tall and straight and neatly planted, moonlight filtering through fringed branches, land opening up on either side, manicured lawns and sculpted hedges and beautiful rose-gardens just visible beyond the further edges of the estate.

Vicky cleared her throat, said, 'How pretty . . .'

and then gasped as Callicoe House came into view.

It was breathtaking. The Elizabethan manor sprawled in elegant disarray, with chimneys like barley sticks, long dark wooden beams, criss-cross red bricks and pretty lattice windows, all gleaming softly under the moon, a weathercock perched in silhouette against that blue and white sky. There were outhouses and stables to the left, a vast towering oak to the right, and, parked in front of the house, a long, elegant dark blue limousine.

Vicky stared at it in total silence, eyes wide.

Scott parked beside his mother's limousine. 'No mistakes, Vicky,' he said tightly, watching her. 'Not with my mother.'

She looked at him angrily through her dark lashes. 'Give me a chance, Scott. I haven't even met her yet. I can handle it—you don't have to keep on at me.'

He got out of the car, and after a moment Vicky followed him. The front door was arched oak and ivy grew up the wall beside it in twists and green tangles.

'Scott, how lovely to see you again.' Emmy Crowsal looked just like her husband, tall and slim and cheerful, with dark hair and blue eyes which flickered over Vicky with bright, curious interest. 'This the young lady?'

Scott turned to Vicky, his eyes hard. 'Isn't she gorgeous?' He slid a hand around Vicky's waist, his fingers pressing a warning. 'Tom told me she was home . . .?'

'Caterina?' Emmy nodded. 'Yes, she's in her bedroom. I'll settle you in the drawing-room, and go and tell her you're here.'

The drawing-room was so exquisitely decorated that Vicky could only walk through it and stare, seeing the French brocade chairs, the gilt mirror, the antique tables, the elegant portraits on the walls, some modern art, various books, family photographs in the corner.

'That's my father,' Scott said, watching her as she stopped to look at a large black and white photograph of a very handsome, austere man in his fifties.

Vicky nodded. 'What was his name?'

'David.'

She put the photograph down, picked up another.

'That's me,' Scott drawled, smiling, 'in New York.'

'I would never have guessed,' Vicky said, tongue in cheek, and he came to stand beside her, looking down at himself as a young man, wearing jeans and a leather jacket, standing on a ship's deck with New York sprawling behind him like the jagged teeth of some twentieth-century monster.

'I was twenty-one,' he said, smiling.

Vicky nodded, tears springing unbidden and certainly unwanted to her eyes. Irritably, she put the photograph down and folded her arms. 'I thought your mother was expecting us,' she said with a snap.

'She's always fashionably late,' remarked Scott, and at that moment the door opened.

Caterina Thornton came in, a gracious smile on her fine-boned face as she said, 'Darling . . . so sorry I'm late . . . lovely to see you,' and looked at her son through her eyelashes as she waited for her kiss.

'Hello,' Scott said softly, brushing his mouth against her scented cheek. 'You're looking as wonderful as ever.' The grey eyes flickered over her. 'I like your hair . . .is it a new style?'

Caterina patted her hair, the grey curls soft and perfectly cut around her delicate face, large grey eyes expertly made-up, her clothes elegant and feminine. The black dress was obviously Chanel, the gold earrings and necklace and bracelet echoing Vicky's in a way which made Vicky feel horribly self-conscious, convinced the other woman looked better than her.

'Yes, darling, it is new,' Caterina was saying. 'I had to wait ages at the salon, though . . . I hope they're not going to make a habit of it.' The serene grey eyes alighted on Vicky and she smiled graciously. 'You must be Victoria. Hello, it's lovely to meet you . . .'

Vicky gave a nervous smile. 'Yes, how do you do, Mrs Thornton . . .' she said, tripping over the words.

'Oh, please,' smiled Caterina, 'call me Caterina.'

'Thank you,' Vicky stammered.

'Do sit down.' Caterina moved to the bell-pull with a smile. 'Emmy will get drinks for us. What would you like?'

Later, they ate dinner in the long dining-room. Vicky was under terrible strain, flirting with Scott, watching him flirt with his mother, and watching his mother control the proceedings with that serene, self-assured smile.

'Of course, when David was alive,' Caterina was saying wistfully, 'we celebrated our wedding anniversary by throwing a party here, every year, just as though it was the wedding all over again.'

Vicky smiled, touched. 'It must have been a very happy marriage.'

'Oh, yes.' Caterina's lashes flickered; she looked beautiful in the soft light from the candelabra, her eyes iridescent. 'David and I were in love till the end.'

There was a little silence.

Caterina cleared her throat. 'Scott flies me to Paris every year instead, now.' She smiled at Scott through her lashes. 'Dinner at Maxim's . . . it was David's favourite restaurant.'

'I'm not surprised,' Vicky said with a light laugh. 'My father took me there on a trip to Paris when I was a child. It's beautiful, isn't it?'

'Did he really, Victoria?' Caterina studied her across the table. 'Such a sweet man . . . I was so sorry to hear about his heart attack. Scott sent flowers for me—did they arrive, darling?' She turned to her son, brows raised.

'I delivered them personally,' Scott drawled, leaning back in his chair, one hand in the pocket of his grey suit, the jacket falling open to reveal that powerful chest, his smile as he watched Vicky across the table making her heart race. If only he meant it. If only he looked at her like that more often.

'That was kind of you,' Vicky said huskily to him, looking at him through her dark lashes.

Scott smiled lazily, ran a hand through his dark hair.

'That's OK.'

She flushed unaccountably, heart racing. It felt so intimate, even though his mother was there; it felt as though he really meant all of this—the way he was talking to her, smiling at her, touching her every now and then. It was hard to remind herself that it was a show put on for his mother.

Caterina cleared her throat. 'Shall we call Emmy to clear away dinner?'

Scott got to his feet. 'I'll call her . . .' He went to the bell-pull, smiled at his mother, and she smiled back.

'I understand it's to be December the first?' Caterina said as they sat once more in the drawing-room, drinking coffee from elegant French cups.

'Yes,' Vicky said, 'in the private chapel.'

Caterina nodded. 'I remember your father's wedding. It was held there, too.'

Vicky's brows shot up. 'Did you attend?'

'Oh, yes, of course.' Caterina smiled serenely. 'David and I were both there. We knew your parents very well then.'

'I was there, too, Vicky,' Scott drawled, and she looked up in astonishment. 'I was about twelve, I think,' he continued. 'I don't remember very much . . . your mother looked beautiful—I remember that . . .'

'Oh, radiant,' agreed Caterina, 'but she always was. A real beauty, Victoria. And so stylish.'

Vicky studied her, touched beyond words. It was the first time anyone had spoken of her mother with admiration or pleasure. Vicky always felt condemned, not flattered, to resemble her. But as she met Caterina's soft grey eyes she saw the smile in them, and she smiled back, saying, 'She did look lovely on her wedding day. I saw some photographs . . .'

'A very sensual woman,' Caterina said, watching Vicky across the table. 'And so charming. We both adored her.'

Vicky met Scott's eyes and flushed hotly, bending her head. The clock ticked in the drawing-room, the elegant Louis XV gold copy blending in perfectly with the rest of the room.

As they drove home later, Vicky looked at Scot in the darkened car and said huskily, 'Scott . . . I'm sorry . . . about what I said last night.'

He shot her a cool, frowning glance.

'About Challa,' she said softly, 'about you. I'm sorry.'

He pursed his hard mouth. 'Forget it. I realise Charles put it all in your head. That was obvious from the minute I walked in.'

Vicky flushed, feeling transparent. 'How long have your family lived at that house?' she asked, desperate to change the subject.

'Only two hundred years,' he drawled wryly.

Vicky smiled. 'That's quite a long time.'

He gave a cool laugh. 'Oh, that redeems me, does it?'

Her face fell. 'I didn't say——'

'No,' he said tightly, 'but you implied it!' He changed gear angrily as they turned into the gates of Challa. 'And if your poisonous cousin decides to start spreading the rumour, I'll definitely transfer him to London.' His face was grimly angry. 'Piece by piece.'

She tensed as he jerked the car to a halt and got out, slamming the door behind him. Watching his dark, powerful silhouette disappear through the front door, Vicky exhaled her breath on a shaky sigh.

She followed him in to the drawing-room. 'Look, Scott,' she said as she closed the door behind her, 'Charles won't tell anyone anything. Not with that threat hanging over his head.'

'Oh, great!' he said tightly, brandy glass in hand. 'I take it you don't want him transferred to London?'

'Well,' she said carefully, 'he wouldn't be happy there.'

His smile was all ice. 'And you want Charles to be happy!'

She flushed. 'He's my——'

'Cousin, yes!' he snapped, putting his glass down with a thud. 'So you've said, interminably, every time we mention his name.'

Vicky lifted her chin, angry. 'Jealous, Scott?'

Dark red colour invaded his face. 'No, I am not bloody well jealous!'

She stared, her heart leaping, and said softly, 'Scott . . .?'

Moving shakily across the room, she placed her hand on his expensive grey sleeve. 'Scott, please tell me if——'

'Would you excuse me?' he said without warning, his face absolutely hard, his eyes icy. 'I'm afraid I have to go out in a minute.'

Vicky stopped where she was, frozen, staring. 'But it's nearly midnight——'

'And Annabel is having trouble convincing herself that we've split up,' he said coolly, eyes veiled. 'I promised I'd drive over there after dinner. She'll be alone, don't worry. No one will know. She just needs a little support . . .'

'*I'll* know!' Vicky said tightly, her face white. 'And I won't let you go, Scott.'

He studied her for a second with cool mockery, then laughed. 'You won't let me go . . .' he drawled. 'I see . . .'

Her mouth shook. 'I told you, Scott, your affair with Annabel must end.'

'And I told you,' he said bitingly, 'not to give me orders.'

They faced each other in silence, eyes warring. Vicky's heart was beating fast and hard as she studied that ruthless face and saw no love there, no kindness, just cold, hard determination.

'All right.' She stepped back, shaking, tears burning the back of her eyes, tears she blinked back fiercely. 'Go to her. But if you do, Scott, our engagement is over. Have you go that? It's over. Finished.' She was trembling with unaccountable rage. 'I will not be humiliated by you. Not like this. Not with my own cousin!'

'A shame you didn't have a ring to pull off and throw at me.' He adjusted his tie, drawling unpleasantly, 'So much more effective in a dramatic scene, don't you think?'

With that, he brushed past her and she hated him, glaring at him through a sheen of black tears as he left the room and shut the door behind him. As she heard the engine of the Ferrari roar in the night she knew Scott had won hands down, as he always did, with no effort whatsoever.

He'd be with Annabel in less than twenty minutes. The pain and savage jealousy shot through her in waves and she sank down on to the couch, loathing the silence of Challa, the terrible loneliness she suddenly felt, the lovelessness of everything in her life.

Tears streaked her face; but they were not tears of self-pity. Vicky dashed them away with an angry hand, lifting her head.

She had delivered an ultimatum to him. Vicky knew she was lost if she went back on it. The engagement would have to end now. It was irretrievable. If Scott could behave as he wished, keep his mistresses throughout their marriage . . . well, what was the point in continuing with it, anyway?

He would crucify her if she let him. It would kill her to marry him and watch the women parade in and out of his life. Particularly Annabel. She couldn't take it if it was Annabel he was making love to instead of her.

She couldn't face it. Her mouth crumpled and she put her face in her hands, sobbing.

But what would her father say if she broke off the engagement now? It would be an appalling shock to him; the heart attack might well repeat itself, scandal or no scandal.

Where did that leave her?

Next day, her father came home from hospital. Vicky was glad to see him, her face lighting up as she ran to the car to greet him.

'Scott's hired some dragon to look after me,' he groaned as he walked into the house on her arm. 'It must be revenge for this Paris trip!'

Scott laughed, carrying his suitcase in. 'Paris is always a pleasure.'

'Is Caroline going with you?' James asked, and Vicky tensed, immediately thinking, Caroline?

Who on earth is Caroline?

'Yes,' Scott said coolly. 'She always accompanies me on these trips now. I find her quite irreplaceable.'

'She's a damned fine secretary,' said James, and Vicky felt jealous although she kept her face cool, deliberately not speaking to Scott or even looking at him. She had heard him come in at three a.m. and she had dark circles under her eyes to prove it.

Scott was barely speaking to her, either. If her father noticed the atmosphere, he said nothing.

'What's she like?' Vicky asked casually later as she played chess with her father before dinner that night. 'Scott's secretary?'

'Smart businesswoman.' James moved a knight forwards. 'Blonde, early thirties, drives a little red sports car.'

'Was she your secretary before Scott arrived?' Vicky studied the board, although her mind was not on the game and the pieces swam before her eyes.

'No, no,' said James. 'Scott hired her himself about a year ago.'

Vicky looked at the clock above the fireplace and thought of him at work, feet up on the desk as he watched the blonde, beautiful Caroline swaying in some glamorous outfit, pad and pencil in hand.

He got home at nine, and dinner was held for him. Vicky watched him burst into the dining-room like a conquering hero, flinging his silk-lined jacket on to a chair, sitting down at the head of the table in black waistcoat and pale shirt and dark red silk tie.

'Sorry I'm late,' he drawled as Mrs Wendle served soup from a large tureen. 'Hectic day at the office.'

James broke his roll with lean fingers. 'I had a lovely call from your mother today, Scott. She's as pleased as I am by this marriage.'

Scott smiled, nodding. 'Vicky and I dined there last night.' He shot a cold warning glance at Vicky which she deliberately ignored, her face haughty and cold.

'So Caroline told me,' he said, and gave Vicky an odd look, frowning. 'Why didn't you mention it to me, darling?'

Vicky flushed, avoiding Scott's eyes. 'It slipped my mind . . .' she said huskily. 'I was so pleased you were home, Daddy . . .'

Later, when her father had been ordered to bed by his nurse, an attractive red-haired divorcee with a firm manner and bright smile, Scott kept Vicky in the drawing-room when she tried to go to bed at the same time as her father.

'No,' he said, watching her steel-eyed as she rose, 'you've got some explaining to do.'

'Such as?' she asked flatly, her face hostile.

'Such as why you didn't mention that dinner,' he drawled, walking coolly towards her. 'Any woman in love would have been delighted to meet her prospective mother-in-law.' His eyes were narrowed and hard. 'You must stay in character, Vicky, or he'll guess.'

Her mouth tightened. 'But I'm not a woman in love,' she said angrily. 'Am I?' She turned to leave the room, but his hand caught her arm with an angry bite.

'Don't you walk away when I'm talking to you!' he said under his breath.

'Why not?' she said tightly. 'It's about time someone did.'

His hand bit into her wrist. 'Meaning?'

'Meaning that you think you're some kind of a god around here!' Her eyes flashed sparks of temper at him. 'Walking in as if you already own the place, sitting at the head of the table while my father's there, ordering us all around——'

'Ordering *you* around,' he said, malice glittering in his eyes, 'which in my opinion is something you need.'

'Nobody wants your opinion!' she flung. 'And I certainly don't want your company!' Scathingly, she ran her eyes over his lean, powerful figure. 'Why don't you run off to Annabel if you want a little hero-worship? Or maybe your beautiful blonde secretary might oblige!'

His hard mouth twisted in a sardonic smile. 'Now *you* sound jealous,' he drawled.

'Not jealous,' she said fiercely, her face running with hot colour, 'furious! I heard you come in at three in the morning. Do you think I'm deaf? I should think the whole town knew you were out with Annabel. Mrs Wendle must certainly suspect!'

'Mrs Wendle is *paid* to be discreet,' he said tightly.

'And how much must I pay *you*,' she said tightly, 'to match her discretion?'

His smile was barbed. 'I'll take your body as a down payment.'

She caught her breath, staring at him, her face flooding with violent colour.

He nodded, eyes narrowing, slipping to her breasts, full and softly outlined in the white silk dress that clung to her curves like a second skin. 'I thought that would shut you up,' he drawled softly. 'Sex invariably does.'

'You're disgusting!' she said fiercely, and he laughed angrily.

'You didn't say that when I had you on the floor the other night. Or on the couch. Or even in the bedroom.' The grey eyes glittered with carefully controlled rage. 'In fact, you were more than willing to——'

'Don't dredge that up,' she floundered, heart thudding at the memory, overwhelmingly aware of how close he was to her and hating herself for the sheer sexual excitement that she felt when he so much as spoke to her. 'We're talking about you and your mistress now! Not some ancient event I can't even remember!'

His mouth tightened. 'Perhaps I should refresh your memory, then . . .' He jerked her towards him and she struggled, fiercely angry, humiliated by his confidence that she would capitulate under sexual pressure.

'Don't touch me!' she cried out breathlessly, hands pushing hard on his broad shoulders as he pulled her towards him. 'Go to Annabel! Go to Caroline! Go to anyone, but just don't come to me! I can't stand to have you touch me—do you hear?'

Rage leapt from his eyes. 'You lying little bitch! You go up in flames every time I kiss you! Do you think I can't feel your response?' His hand shot to her breast and she caught her breath, heart thudding violently. 'You see?' he said thickly, grey eyes staring at her mouth. 'Your body gives you away, Vicky. Listen to that heartbeat . . .'

'It's fear, Scott,' she said lightly, forcing herself to remain calm, not to struggle as his hand slid caressingly over her breast, the nipple hardening under his fingers. Sexual excitement rose up in her and she let it come, enjoying the feel of his hand under her breast, unable to stop that one instinctive reaction, but equally unable to show it. 'It's just fear that make me react like that.'

He gave a harsh crack of laughter. 'You must think I was born yesterday!' He was breathing hard, his face dark with anger: 'How many women do you think there have been, Vicky? In Paris, New York, London, Rome . . . do you think I've gone around with my eyes closed all this time? Do you think I can't tell the difference?'

'Obviously not!' She was desperate not to give

in and make a fool of herself. 'Or you'd know I found your attentions distasteful.'

His mouth was white with rage. 'Distasteful?'

'Yes . . .' she stammered huskily, staring, 'distasteful——'

'All right,' he said bitingly, 'in that case, you certainly won't object if I go to see Annabel, will you?'

Vicky swayed, her face white. 'No,' she said stiffly. 'Not at all.'

He watched her for a second, then slammed out of the room, and Vicky subsided on to the couch, weeping. She was suddenly horrified at the prospect of facing this marriage, facing this kind of scene night after night, watching him run to the arms of another woman, leaving her alone and miserable in this great silent house.

Suddenly, she couldn't stand it any longer. She heard his car flare down the driveway at top speed, and it was at that point that she decided to follow him.

She had to. She had to stop this affair with Annabel or the marriage she was now forced to go through with would destroy her.

Running into the hall, she slipped on her coat, felt in the pocket for the keys to the Rolls, then quickly ran outside into the darkened grounds and got behind the wheel.

If her father had heard any of that, there was nothing she could do about it. Vicky flared the engine, shot away down the drive, suddenly filled with courage and a sense of purpose as she headed out across the darkened countryside for Foxdale Hall.

At some point, approaching the hall from the south, she felt her heart start to thud with nerves. What would he say if she rolled up at this time of night, following him to his mistress's house?

Vicky stopped outside the gates to the hall and sat in the darkness for some time, warring with her pride and her anger, telling herself constantly that this had to be done, she had to stop the affair before anyone found out . . .

But all the time she knew her real reason for being there, her real reason for sitting outside Foxdale Hall at midnight, alone in a darkened Rolls-Royce, terrified to drive in and complete her journey.

She was head over heels in love with him.

It knifed through her and she actually groaned, closing her eyes, unable to move for twenty long seconds as she sat in silence and faced it, faced it all, all the long weeks of trying to win, trying to put him in his place, trying to stop *him* winning, playing endless, complicated games with him, matching him, fighting him, rejecting him, hating him, laughing with him . . . loving him.

A sigh broke her lips as she opened her eyes and looked at the silent grounds of Foxdale Hall. I'm in love with him, she thought, and suddenly wanted to cry.

I'm in love with him . . . And Scott seemed to

open out in her mind like a long, preordained road
with signposts and crossroads, and, thinking about
it, she felt such a deep sense of rightness that she
was shaken by the depth of her emotions.

In her mind's eyes she saw him making love to
Annabel, right now, in the drawing-room of the
hall; she saw the hard, determined face, the
ambition which had taken him from that beautiful,
elegant Elizabethan home in the countryside as a
young man to New York, to Wall street, to success
and money and power. The young man who had
hung around Challa on his black motorbike had
wanted Challa—but only on his terms. Only as a
conquering hero. And only for himself. She
wondered if he wanted it in order to match that
giant father who towered in Caterina's mind as so
irreplaceable, and no doubt towered in Scott's
mind as a shadow to be matched, length for length,
eyeball to eyeball. He'd done it. He didn't really
need Challa to complete his victory over himself
and his image of perfection. His success was in
him, it was written on every line of that hard,
commanding face, in every step he took, his walk
so self-assured and authoritative that nobody
could doubt the man he was.

Tears scalded her cheeks as she sat in the silent
car and faced it. Scott really had won everything
this time; but he must never know. At all costs, he
must never know, Vicky thought fiercely.

She looked at the gates and lifted her chin. If she
went in now it would be the end. Scott would

immediately guess at the real reasons for following him. He would know as soon as he looked at her. He would know she was in love with him, and that final humiliation was more than Vicky could bear.

Resigned, she leant forwards and started the car, pulling away quietly, making a U-turn outside those beautiful white gates and driving back towards Challa.

She thought she'd lie awake, unable to sleep, waiting for him to come home. But perhaps expecting insomnia gave her a reprieve, and she fell asleep quite quickly.

Some time in the night, though, she jerked awake, hearing a crash from the bedroom next door. Alert, anxious, she scanned her dark bedroom as she listened for another noise, a sign that nothing had happened, that Scott was OK.

When there was silence, she hesitated, pulses skipping at the fear of being made to look a fool, then got out of bed and slipped on her red silk négligé over her red silk nightie before padding out of her room and listening at Scott's door.

There was total silence. Heart thudding, she tapped on the door, and whispered, 'Scott . . .?'

There was no reply. Tentatively, Vicky opened the door. The room was in darkness. She could smell whisky. Frowning, she moved inside, a hand reaching out to switch on the light.

'Don't touch that switch!' Scott's voice sliced across the room at her and she froze, peering into the bedroom.

'Scott?' Her eyes could barely adjust to the dark. 'Are you OK?'

His laugh was low, evil, frightening. 'Oh,' he said softly, 'I'm just fine . . . just fine!'

She swallowed, hesitating. 'I . . . I heard a crash . . .'

'So you thought you'd come in here in your sexy nightdress and give me a thrill,' he drawled, and she suddenly saw the glitter of his grey eyes. He was standing by the window, leaning on it, and a bottle of whisky was in his hand. 'Well, that's very kind of you, Vicky. I could do with a thrill. Why don't you step inside and shut the door.'

She said stiffly, 'I just wanted to check you were OK. I didn't realise you were in such a filthy mood.' She started to close the door when he moved, and she froze at the sound of his heavy, clumsy movements, suddenly realising that he was very drunk.

'No don't go,' he said with lazy menace, and as he stepped into the light from the landing she saw with a shock that his hair was tousled, his face flushed with alcohol, his chest completely bare, the hairs rough on its bronzed, muscled surface, a slim line of hair leading down over and under his navel. He wore only a pair of black trousers, his feet quite bare. 'I was just sitting here, thinking about you, Vicky . . .' He laughed softly, his eyes hostile. 'About how much I'm looking forward to our wedding night——'

Vicky backed away instinctively. 'You're drunk, Scott——'

His hand caught her wrist bitingly. 'That's right,' he said tightly, dragging her inside the dark room and closing the door. 'I'm absolutely smashed out of my head.'

'Let me put the light on,' she said, panic rising in her like a flood-tide.

'I don't think so,' he drawled, his eyes glittering in the darkness. 'Not just yet, not before I've told you how I see our wedding night.' He laughed, moving closer, pressing her against the back of the door. 'Do you want to know how I see our wedding night, darling?'

Her heart was thudding with fear and excitement. 'No, I——'

'I'll bet you don't!' he whispered thickly, violence bristling from him as he pressed her against the door. 'I'll bet you don't want to even think about it, so *distasteful* are my attentions to you!'

She caught her breath on a raw gasp. 'I didn't mean that,' she stammered, desperate to get away from him, sensing the violence in him as very real. 'I said it because I don't want to go to bed with you before the wedding.'

'You don't want to go to bed with me at all,' he bit out.

She flushed. 'I . . .'

'And you really expect me to marry you under those circumstances?' he said tightly.

'We have no choice,' she said breathlessly; oh, God, his chest was bare beneath her hands, she could smell his skin, his hair, feel his breathing against her white face. 'You know that as well as I do.'

'You frigid little bitch!' he said hoarsely. 'What are you going to do on the wedding night? Lie back and think of Challa?'

She caught her breath at the insult, furious. '*You* want Challa; not me!' she flung fiercely. 'I don't need to want it! It's mine already!'

He gave a low howl of rage, caught her hair in his hand and tugged it painfully, whispering, 'I don't want your bloody house! I want to know I'm not marrying an iceberg!'

She whimpered, her head thrown back, staring into his dark, ruthless face. 'I'll be ready when the time comes . . .'

'You'll be ready now, you little bitch!' he said hoarsely, and then his mouth was at her throat, sucking hungrily, moaning as she gasped involuntarily, her hands sliding over his shoulders as she gave in to the weakness she knew she couldn't fight. She shuddered as his hands ran over her body, relishing his fierce intake of breath as he sensed her sudden, sharp excitement. His mouth suddenly crushed hers beneath it as he released her hair, his hands sliding to her breasts, pushing the négligé aside, then the bodice of the nightdress, before his mouth fastened hotly over her nipple, and she started to moan, stroking his hair, whispering his name, her mind flying out of her grasp as she allowed her sexuality to take over. 'Oh, God, yes . . .' he muttered thickly, and her heart skipped several beats as she melted against him like a fool, blind to all reason.

Then suddenly she was shoved aside, and her startled eyes stared at him, confused and at a loss, her faced flushed with excitement.

'My God!' he said hoarsely, staring at her. 'You really are an expert, aren't you?'

'I . . .' She could barely speak, her confusion too great. She was still caught up in the excitement of being able to revel in his touch.

'An expert, Vicky,' he said tightly, 'at making men make fools of themselves over you.'

Vicky looked at him in silence for a long, painful moment. For a second she thought she hadn't heard him correctly. She just stood very still, hardly daring to breathe, her eyes running over his silhouette, the gleam of his skin, his height, his grey eyes.

'What did you say?' she asked breathlessly.

His eyes were bleak. He studied her in the darkness for a moment, then turned away. 'Nothing.'

She swallowed, her throat dry as ashes, and reached out a hand. 'Scott . . .?'

He leapt away from her, eyes flashing silver. 'I said nothing!' he bit out. 'Are you deaf?' His mouth tightened, and he suddenly shot forwards, hands gripping her upper arms as he shook her violently, eyes blazing. 'What are you hanging around for? Do you want to get yourself raped?'

'No!' she cried out as he shook her, staring at him in wide-eyed fear.

'Then I suggest,' he said through his teeth, opening the door, 'that you don't come to my bedroom in the early hours of the morning dressed like a whore!'

Vicky stood on the threshold of his bedroom, eyes black with hatred and filled with angry tears.

'You bastard!' she said under her breath, shaking with anger.

He laughed harshly. 'Yes, that's right, Vicky,' he drawled, eyes hating her. 'I'm beginning to think you and I really are well-matched!'

The door slammed in her face. She stared at it, beside herself with fury and hurt pride for a moment, and considered hurling herself at it, kicking and punching it and waking the whole house up . . .

Her mouth tightened. She went back to her own room and slammed the door, unable to stop shaking as she thought of the things he'd said. How could he say them to her? How could he? Frigid. . . he'd accused her of being frigid! Her hands shook as she sat on the bed, clutching the coverlet.

At least she had the consolation of knowing he hadn't guessed. He hadn't suspected for a minute that she was now in love with him. How easy it would have been for her to give that away . . . how easy . . . She remembered her feelings as he'd kissed her throat . . . yes, it would have been very easy to just blurt it out in a rush of emotion and excitement. But at least she had that to hold on to.

In my lonely bed, she thought, and turned on to her face, tears scalding her cheeks as she listened to the silence and felt the aching loneliness in that silent, clifftop bedroom.

Outside, the wind was rising, and the trees were swaying softly as it rose. Tomorrow there would be a storm. Gulls would fly inland, the skies would be grey and depressing, the sea would fight the land in grey-white flashes of foam.

Vicky felt lonelier than she ever had in her life before.

CHAPTER TEN

NEXT day, Vicky had dark circles under her eyes again. Scott was at the dining-table for breakfast with her father, and they both looked up as she came in.

'Good morning, darling,' James offered his handsome cheek for a kiss. 'Didn't you sleep well?'

Vicky felt herself blush, kissing her father and saying huskily, 'No . . . I suppose it was the moon.'

'Female nonsense!' her father snorted, flicking *The Times* in his hands. 'It's just superstition, Vicky. The moon has no effect on our lives whatsoever, and anyone who believes otherwise is in need of a lobotomy.'

Scott laughed, his eyes never moving from the pages of the *Financial Times*.

Vicky sat down and spooned some scrambled eggs on to her plate. 'I read an article the other day that said the moon has a very strong effect——'

'In a women's magazine, no doubt,' said her father.

Vicky decided to give up that particular conversation.

'Scott didn't sleep very well either,' James said with a sudden frown, and as Vicky looked up so did Scott, and their eyes met with a sudden jolt of realisation across the table.

There was a short, tense silence. Vicky's fork hovered in suspension over her eggs as she tried to think of something to say to cover her father's suspicions.

'We stayed up,' Scott said suddenly, coolly, 'after you'd gone to bed.' The grey eyes were riveted on Vicky. 'Didn't we, darling?'

James looked at her closely.

She blushed, saying huskily, 'Well, not for very long . . .'

James laughed, relaxing. 'Thank goodness for that. I thought you'd had a row or something.'

'Why on earth should you think that?' Scott drawled, leaning back in his chair, hands behind his dark head.

'Well, ' James frowned, shifting, 'you don't spend very much time together. I suppose it's the office, of course; forgive me, Scott.'

Scott watched Vicky and she watched him. Her father was no fool. Her would guess very quickly that this was likely to be an unhappy marriage, and that would kill him.

'We've got to do something,' Scott told her deeply as she followed him out into the hall after breakfast. 'If he guesses what's really going on, it'll kill him. He's pinning everything on this marriage, Vicky.'

'It might help if you didn't keep driving over to Annabel's every night,' she said tightly.

The grey eyes narrowed. 'Are you prepared to

take her place?'

Vicky looked away. 'No!'

'Then stop asking me to give her up!' The biting tone was almost a whisper as they stood close together in the hall, keeping their voices down.

'I see,' Vicky said after a moment, her throat tight with pain. 'That's your price, is it?'

He studied her coldly. 'Take it or leave it.'

Bitterness filled her eyes. 'You know very well I can't take it!'

'No, I don't,' he said tightly. 'I only know that you refuse.'

Her mouth trembled. She looked away, took a deep breath and said shakily, 'Scott, I can't go to bed with you. You don't love me. I——'

'Oh, God,' he drawled, 'don't drag love into it. It's so boringly irrelevant!'

Vicky looked at him with black hatred in her eyes. Then, angrily, she pushed past him.

His hands caught her arm. 'I'm sorry,' he said under his breath, mouth hard. 'Look—we haven't got time to go through all this right now. We've got to think of a way to convince your father that——'

'That we're in love?' she said scathingly.

He had the good grace to redden. 'Yes,' he said, releasing her arm.

Vicky looked him over with cold, hostile eyes. 'You're the ideas man. You're the whizz-kid. You think of something.'

'All right,' he said, mouth tightening, 'I will.'

He glanced at his watch. 'I'll work myself into the ground and get off at two. We'll go out for the afternoon. To my mother's. You can ride, or something—anything. Just so long as James believes we're rushing off to spend a rapturous afternoon together.'

'Oh, that'll really convince him,' she said tightly, 'when you disappear at midnight again tonight!'

His eyes flashed. 'Will you stop trying to destroy this whole——' He broke off as the dining-room door opened, and the next minute his mouth was clamped hard against hers in a burning kiss that knocked her off her feet, made her cling to his shoulders with a muffled gasp. She heard her father walk out into the hall, see them embracing passionately, see the heightened colour of Scott's dark face, and then laugh softly, disappearing into the drawing-room.

Scott pulled away from her immediately.

Vicky swayed, dazed by his kiss, struggling to readjust her attitude to one of dislike. 'I . . . that was quick thinking, Scott . . .' she said huskily, not looking at him. 'I'm sure that's put his mind at rest.'

Scott ran a shaking hand through his hair. 'Yes . . .' He swung his jacket over one broad shoulder, lashes flickering as he looked away, his face flushed. 'I'll see you at two o'clock.'

Vicky watched him walk out of the front door, her eyes drinking in every detail of him, the tilt of his dark head as he walked, the width of his shoulders, the long, lean legs, the way his dark hair lifted as the morning breeze rippled the land.

Oh, God, how much longer could she keep this up?

She spent the morning with her father and his nurse, Diana Morton, who kept him fully occupied, her manner slightly flirtatious and very charming. Vicky was most amused watching them play chess together, noting the quick upward looks Diana gave him from beneath her starched white cap, and the answering smiles James threw her across the chessboard.

Daddy, flirting? Vicky thought, amused. Heavens, no! She hadn't seem him flirt for years—except with her. Her eyes widened as she looked at her father's austere silver head . . . he'd always flirted with her. He'd flirted with her all her life. How could she have believed he didn't love her?

At lunchtime, a car drew up outside and Vicky rushed to the front door, thinking Scott must be early.

'Hello, darling!' Uncle William hovered on the doorstep and as Vicky stared at him in surprise she saw Sylvia's blonde head behind him, and then Annabel's dark one . . . the flash of jealousy was so severe she was almost knocked backwards by it. 'Is James up and about? We brought some flowers and chocolate. . . hope we're not intruding . . .?'

Vicky stepped back, ashen, stiff with self-control. 'Of course not,' she said politely, burning with rage as she met Annabel's proud, beautiful stare. 'Do come in. I'm sure he'll be delighted to see you.'

Stiffly, she led the way to the drawing-room. 'Daddy,' she said in a stilted voice, 'look who's come to see you.'

James looked up from the chessboard. 'William! Lovely to see you, old chap! How are you?'

Vicky couldn't face sitting with them all. Seeing Annabel was like having a knife pushed into her heart. All she could think of was Scott and her, together, lovers . . . were they in love? Her whole life tasted suddenly of ashes as that thought hit her. Not Annabel, she thought, heart aching; don't let him be in love with her.

'Reckon they want lunch, don't you?' Mrs Wendle said irritably when she told her who'd arrived.

'I think that's the general idea.' Vicky nibbled on a raw carrot as she perched on a stool in the airy blue and white tiled kitchen.

'Good job I'm such an imaginative cook,' said Mrs Wendle with a smile. 'It's very short notice, if you ask me. Look at the time! Close to one o'clock!'

'Something light will be fine,' Vicky said.

'Yes,' agreed Mrs Wendle, 'and a few extra pats of butter for Miss Annabel's plate.'

Vicky looked at her sharply. 'Wendle!' She laughed, catching the twinkle in Mrs Wendle's eyes. 'That was a very naughty thing to say!'

Mrs Wendle chuckled. 'Very naughty!' Her brows rose at Vicky. 'Six extra pats? Or seven?'

Vicky roared with laughter and left the kitchen in a better mood, preparing herself to go and face lunch with her relatives, which wasn't an easy task.

'. . . so pleased to hear about Scott and Vicky,' William was saying later as they ate salmon steaks with salad in the dining-room. 'Such a perfect match . . .'

Annabel watched Vicky across the polished mahogany dining-table and Vicky felt the knives in her green eyes shooting across at her all through lunch.

It was a struggle to hide her jealousy. A struggle, but sheer pride kept it at bay as she spoke politely to Annabel, her face a cool mask, haughty and impenetrable.

After lunch, Vicky excused herself from the drawing-room to go up and change for her afternoon with Scott.

In her bedroom, she stripped and showered quickly, tugging on black jodhpurs and a white blouse, a hacking jacket and a black hair-net covering her silky black hair. She placed the black velvet riding hat on her head and surveyed her cool reflection with bitterness.

No one would guess from looking at her that she

was not a radiant bride. Only the tell-tale bloodshot redness of her eyes gave away her true state of emotional despair.

The knock at her door made her jump.

'Come in!' she called, trembling, expecting to see Scott.

It was Annabel.

Vicky stared, taken aback. 'Why, Annabel,' she said huskily, stammeringly, 'what brings you up here?'

Annabel closed the door, her green eyes bright with jealousy. 'You really think you're something, don't you, Vicky?' she said in a tight, furious little voice.

Vicky blanched, horrified at the prospect of this confrontation, her voice saying politely, 'I really don't know what you're talking about, Annab——'

'Yes, you do, you spoilt little bitch!' Annabel said fiercely, and Vicky's hair stood on end as she stared at her, white-faced. 'You've always had it all, haven't you? From the minute you were born you were always the favourite. Vicky must have this and Vicky must have that—and you got it, didn't you?'

Vicky started to laugh, frightened and appalled, and unable to believe what she was hearing, her laughter a product of sheer nerves, not amusement.

'Don't laugh at me!' Annabel said in a high shaking voice. 'You've taken everything! I thought when you left that I'd get Challa! I thought

Scott would marry me and you'd stay away and I'd have——'

'Don't talk to me about Scott!' Vicky hissed suddenly, her jealousy now blazing from her eyes as she faced her cousin. 'He's going to be my husband! I don't want to know about your sordid little affair with him!'

Annabel crimsoned. 'What affair?' she flung bitterly. 'You've put a stop to that, haven't you? It only took you a few short weeks! You just walked in and snatched him from under my nose!'

Vicky stared at her, suddenly silenced by her words and the anger she spoke with. Very slowly, she heard herself say, her chest hurting, 'What do you mean, put a stop to it?' She stared at her cousin. 'When did it stop?'

Annabel looked confused. 'You know when . . . you were there . . .'

Vicky's mouth was dry. 'At the lunch? On Sunday?'

'Yes . . .' Annabel nodded slowly, frowning.

'You mean . . .' Vicky's heart hammered into life, her voice hoarse as she said fiercely, 'you mean you haven't seen Scott since then?'

Annabel just stared at her.

Outside, they both heard a footfall. Scott! Vicky's heart leapt and as it did she put everything together, piece by piece, suddenly feeling it all landslide into place, seeing that he had matched her feelings along the way, that his anger and fierce desire and savage rages could only mean one thing.

He was in love with her.

'Scott!' she cried out without thinking, and then she was running, pushing past Annabel, running out into the corridor, hearing Scott running down the stairs, following him, her heart thumping, pinning everything on her instincts, knowing she was right—he loved her—and refusing to give in to the terrible doubt she felt.

'Scott, wait!' Breathless, she was out in the sunshine, the storm whipping up around Challa, Scott bending to unlock the car door, his dark hair flicking around his tanned face. 'Don't go . . . not like this . . .'

He unlocked the car door, held it with white-knuckled hands, stared at the wheel, didn't move a muscle.

Trembling, she went towards him and put a hand on his stiff, unmoving arm. 'Scott . . .' she said huskily, staring at his averted head, 'Scott . . .' The words dried on her tongue. Suddenly, she wasn't so sure.

'Well?' he said thickly. 'Get on with it.' The dark head lifted and pride blazed in the grey eyes. 'I heard it, Vicky. I heard what she said to you.'

Her heart missed a beat. 'That you didn't go to see her . . .' she whispered. 'Where do you go, Scott?'

He watched her, his eyes bleak, his mouth hard.

'Where?' she said huskily, then on a note of pain, 'To Caroline?'

His dark brows jerked together. 'Caroline?'

'Yes,' she said tightly. 'I know about her.'

He stared at her as if she were mad. 'Caroline is my secretary, Vicky. And believe me, her husband would kill me if I turned up on his doorstep at midnight.'

She blinked rapidly. 'Then where do you go?'

There was a long silence. Scott looked away. The wind ravaged his hair, his black suit, the jacket flying apart, dark red silk tie flickering.

He slammed the car door. 'Nowhere,' he said flatly, 'I just . . . drive. Sometimes I stop the car and walk.' He laughed, grey eyes hard as she looked at her and said flatly, 'Satisfied? Got everything you need now?'

'Need?' she echoed, dazed. 'I don't understand . . .'

He leant towards her, biting out thickly, 'To put the final pieces together, Vicky. To get the full picture.'

She stared at him, her mouth open.

'Don't look at me like that,' he ground out. 'You know damned well I'm in love with you! If you hadn't figured it out before, you must know it now! Especially after that revealing little scene with Annabel!' He turned away from her, his face taut with anger and pride. 'My God, it's even a relief to have said it!'

Vicky couldn't breathe properly, her heart thudding as she stared at him. She knew she would remember every inch of him as he looked today, now, this minute, as he told her he was in love with her; she would remember it for the rest of her life. It was so vivid. So clear. His eyes were so grey, his mouth so hard and proud, the tilt of his dark head telling her he refused to be ruled by his emotions, that he would never give in to her against his better judgement, no matter how deeply he was in love with her. And as she saw all of that in his dark face she felt the tears sting the back of her eyes, heard herself say shakily, 'Darling . . . darling . . .' and then her arms were around him, her face at his throat, breathing in the clean windswept smell of his hair and skin while he stood stock-still, didn't move a muscle.

'Don't,' he said under his breath, and unclasped her hands from the back of his neck, putting her away from him. 'It doesn't change a thing. Not a damned thing. I didn't want to fall in love with you, Vicky, and I don't intend to stay in love with you. It's temporary. It won't last.'

Vicky smiled tremulously, stroking his hair. 'Darling, don't say that . . . I'll die if you stop loving me . . .'

He just stared at her in sudden, still, silence.

'I've been in love with you for weeks,' she said quickly, her eyes wide open. 'Forever, I think.'

'In love with me . . .?'

Vicky nodded, her mouth trembling. 'Desperately.'

He caught her in his arms, pressed her against

him, his mouth at her hair as he said deeply, 'My God, I can't believe it . . .'

'I didn't realise it myself until last night,' she said into his throat, kissing him. 'It was when I followed you to Annabel's——'

'What?' he lifted his head, staring, delighted. 'You followed me?'

Vicky went crimson. 'I hate to admit it, but yes, I did. I didn't dare go in, though. Just sat outside the gates trying to pluck up the courage. I kept telling myself I'd gone there because the scandal of you having an affair with her would be too appalling . . .'

'But you were jealous,' he drawled, smiling. 'I knew you were jealous, I knew it!'

The triumphant ring of his voice made her smile, eyes dancing. 'Don't let it go to your head! It was only a fleeting pang!'

He laughed, gathering her in his arms. 'Oh, God, you've been driving me out of my mind ever since I first set eyes on you in London, Vicky. I was even jealous of that stupid little boy, Spike. When you first arrived back I thought he must be your lover . . . I was thrilled to hear you telling him to get his hands off you.'

She smiled shyly. 'Oh!' The confession made her unexpectedly breathless, suddenly shy, astonished that he could see anything in her.

Scott studied her tenderly. 'And you were so pretty . . .' he stoked her dark hair, 'so incredibly sexy . . . I couldn't believe it was the same little girl I'd known at Challa all those years ago. You hit me like a truck, Vicky. I just looked at your face and fell like a ton of bricks . . .'

'Yes.' She studied him, frowning, a ray of storm-cloud sunlight blinding her suddenly. 'The first moment. I remember it, too. It was so odd . . . like seeing something so overpowering you can't bear to look . . . so you turn your head away . . .'

Scott smiled. 'And pretend not to have seen it.'

Vicky met his eyes and for a moment they were silent, studying one another in the silence that united them for the first time. Vicky felt her mind reach out to his and brush against it, that first tentative touch as hesitant, as exciting as any lover's first kiss.

'Vicky,' Scott said deeply, his hand sliding to her waist as he drew her closer, 'we have a lot of talking to do.'

She nodded, holding him close. 'I'm so glad,' she said huskily, 'so glad we told each other before the wedding.'

He gave a grim smile. 'I know. The thought of it was killing me. I couldn't bear to face it. You would never have seen it, of course, but the pressure was beginning to tell on me.'

'Thank God for Annabel,' she said softly, suddenly remembering that incredible conversation upstairs, all the revelations she had never even guessed at: had Annabel been as jealous of her as she'd been of Annabel all these years? Incredible!

'Yes,' Scott said deeply, 'thank God for Annabel!' He drew back and looked at her, gave a little frown. 'Now,' he drawled, hands sliding to her hips, 'how the hell am I going to peel you out of these jodhpurs?'

Vicky went scarlet, laughing. 'Scott!'

He grinned. 'Let's go to bed!'

She kissed him. 'Not yet.'

'Yes, yet,' he said huskily and bent his head to cover her mouth with a kiss which took her breath away, all the emotion and longing and pent-up desire flaring up between them out of nowhere, leaving them both gasping for breath and flushed in the face, clutching each other as though in danger of drowning. 'Oh, God . . .' Scott dragged his head away from her, his heart thudding under the pale shirt he wore. 'This is too much for me to bear, Vicky. We've got to go to bed, fast, or I'm going to go berserk.'

She looked at him through her dark lashes and said softly, 'What happens when you go berserk?'

A muscle jerked in his cheek. 'Look at me like that,' he said thickly, 'and you'll find out.'

Teasingly, she brushed a kiss on his chest murmuring, 'I wonder what would happen if I started to undo all these buttons.'

He groaned under his breath and whispered, 'Do it, do it, do it!'

Vicky laughed, watching him, and said softly, 'Darling, I love you.'

'But you want to wait until the wedding,' he said

with a resigned sigh. 'Don't tell me, I don't want to hear it!'

'I know,' she said, smiling, 'you want everything at once.'

He caught her hand impulsively and whispered, 'I love to claim my prizes!'

Love rippled through her, and she put her arms around his neck, saying, 'Then claim me darling . . .' Her heart thudded as his mouth came down over hers and the passion flared like wildfire between them.

'Am I winning, Vicky?' he said thickly against her mouth, his hands tight on her hips.

'Yes, darling, winning all the way . . .'

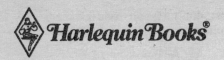
Harlequin Books®

GREAT NEWS...
HARLEQUIN UNVEILS NEW SHIPPING PLANS

For the convenience of customers, Harlequin has announced that Harlequin romances will now be available in stores at these convenient times each month*:

Harlequin Presents, American Romance, Historical, Intrigue:

> May titles: April 10
> June titles: May 8
> July titles: June 5
> August titles: July 10

Harlequin Romance, Superromance, Temptation, Regency Romance:

> May titles: April 24
> June titles: May 22
> July titles: June 19
> August titles: July 24

We hope this new schedule is convenient for you.

With only two trips each month to your local bookseller, you'll never miss any of your favorite authors!

*Please note: There may be slight variations in on-sale dates in your area due to differences in shipping and handling.

*Applicable to U.S. only.

HDATES-RR

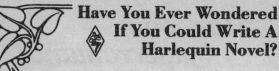

Have You Ever Wondered If You Could Write A Harlequin Novel?

Here's great news—Harlequin is offering a series of cassette tapes to help you do just that. Written by Harlequin editors, these tapes give practical advice on how to make your characters—and your story—come alive. There's a tape for each contemporary romance series Harlequin publishes.

Mail order only

All sales final

- ✂ -

Clip this coupon and return to:

> **HARLEQUIN READER SERVICE**
> Audiocassette Tape Offer
> 3010 Walden Ave.
> P.O. Box 1396
> Buffalo, NY 14269-1396

I enclose my check/money order payable to HARLEQUIN READER SERVICE for $5.70 ($4.95 + 75¢ for delivery) for EACH tape ordered. My total check is for $ _____ .
Please send me:

☐ Romance and Presents   ☐ Intrigue
☐ American Romance   ☐ Temptation
☐ Superromance   ☐ All five tapes ($21.95 total)

Name: _____

Address: _____ Apt: _____

City: _____ State: _____ Zip: _____

NY residents add appropriate sales tax.   AUDIO-H1D

Harlequin Superromance®

Available in Superromance this month
#462—STARLIT PROMISE

STARLIT PROMISE is a deeply moving story of a woman coming to terms with her grief and gradually opening her heart to life and love.

Author Petra Holland sets the scene beautifully, never allowing her heroine to become mired in self-pity. It is a story that will touch your heart and leave you celebrating the strength of the human spirit.

Available wherever Harlequin books are sold.